The Case
of the
Russian
Diplomat

A RINEHART SUSPENSE NOVEL

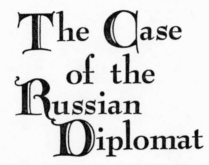

The Case of the Russian Diplomat

A RINEHART SUSPENSE NOVEL

A RINEHART SUSPENSE NOVEL

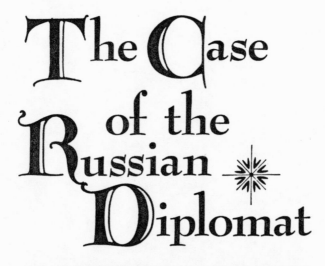

The Case of the Russian Diplomat

A Masao Masuto Mystery
E. V. CUNNINGHAM

HOLT, RINEHART AND WINSTON
New York

1

THE DROWNED MAN

At precisely twenty minutes after three on a Monday morning in November, Detective Sergeant Masao Masuto's telephone rang shrilly, awakening him from an otherwise untroubled sleep. Still half asleep, he pulled the telephone to him and heard Captain Alex Wainwright's rasping voice.

"Masao?"

"I'm here, Captain."

"What in hell are you whispering for? I can't hear you."

"I'm whispering because it's the middle of the night and Kati is asleep."

"I'm not asleep," Kati said.

"I know what time it is," Wainwright snapped. "I'm at the Beverly Glen Hotel, and I want you to get your ass over here. Now."

"Thank you," Masuto said. "You are always considerate of your employees."

"You don't work for me, you work for the city."

Masuto put down the phone, turned on the light, and looked at his wife; he reflected that even awakened rudely from her sleep, Kati managed to give the impression that she had just stepped out of a Japanese print, her black hair held neatly with a ribbon, her face like a lovely, worried ivory cameo.

"Wainwright," Masuto explained.

"I know. I will make hot tea."

"No, no, please. Go back to sleep. He's out of his mind, so there's no time for tea."

But Kati was already out of bed and in her kimono, and before Masuto left the house he had to have the cup of tea and a sweet cake—to raise his blood sugar, as Kati put it. Kati read every article on nutrition that the Los Angeles *Times* printed, and it was her constant grief that away from her, Masuto subsisted on tacos, frankfurters, pizza, and other strange and barbaric concoctions.

In his car, driving north on Motor Road from Culver City, where he lived, to Beverly Hills, Masuto reflected on the fact that he derived so much happiness from a marriage to a very simple and very old-fashioned Japanese woman. Being a Zen Buddhist as well as a member of the Beverly Hills police force, he never confused simplicity with a lack of wisdom; just as being a member of the Beverly Hills police, he never confused wealth with either intelligence or morality. And now as so often before, he congratulated himself on his choice of a mate. He had heard the children whispering as he left the house, awakened by the phone call, and right now Kati would be sitting in their room, singing softly. He smiled at the thought.

During the past ten years, the Beverly Glen Hotel had

"Well, Beckman's no one to talk to about that. Let's see what we got."

It was a clear, cold, moonlit California night, and the pool, lit by its underwater floods, lay in an unreal conglomeration of silver palms, silver awnings, and silver lounge chairs. Seeing was a part of Masuto's religion as well as his way of life. The ugly becomes beautiful, the beautiful ugly and mundane. Someone had once named the pool area of the Beverly Glen Hotel "the naked hooker"; and one day, a few months ago, Masuto had listened to Gellman bewailing the fact that there was no way in the world to rid the hotel of the high-priced call girls who made it their place of business. "The truth is," Gellman had complained, "that there's no way in the world to tell the difference between a guest, a guest's girl, and a hooker. Things have changed." But now the pool area was empty, cold, almost enchanting in the moonlight.

Gellman led the way into the men's locker room. The place was ablaze with light. Stretched out on a bench was the naked body of a man. Dr. Sam Baxter, skinny, normally bad humored, was as annoyed as everyone else at a thing like this taking place in the middle of the night. That made his disposition even worse. He was chief pathologist at All Saints Hospital, doubling as medical examiner in a place where, as he put it, one expects a minimum of violence. He was closing his bag as they entered, and he greeted Masuto with a scowl.

"I'm delighted to see you in good spirits," Masuto said.

Captain Wainwright turned from staring at the body to stare at Masuto. "Hello, Masao," he said, his voice surprisingly mild.

Masuto walked forward and looked at the body. His age, Masuto surmised, was somewhere between fifty and fifty-five. A guess would make him five feet eight inches in height, and he was fat, perhaps two hundred and ten pounds. Thin hair, pasty white skin. Masuto leaned over and lifted one of the corpse's eyelids. The eyes were blue. He touched the eyeball lightly with his thumb and forefinger, and then he peered closely at the small snub nose.

"Maybe I shouldn't have dragged you out of bed," Wainwright said. "No marks on the body. No sign of violence. Sam thinks he drowned."

"I know he drowned," Baxter said sourly.

"You won't know until you do an autopsy," Wainwright said.

"He drowned," Gellman said. "My God, Captain, can't you let it go at that? That's bad enough. We never had a drowning in the pool before."

"Who is he?" Masuto asked.

Wainwright looked at Gellman, who spread his hands and shook his head. "That's it."

"What do you mean, that's it?"

"We don't know who he is," Gellman replied.

"Isn't he a guest?"

"No. At least, we don't think so."

"The daytime room clerk ain't here yet," Comstock explained. "He lives in Pasadena, and he's on his way. But Sal Monti, who runs the parking and who's got a damn good memory, says he's never seen him before. Now that don't mean that he couldn't have got out of a car and come into the hotel when Sal's back was turned. You know how heavy the traffic at the front gets around five o'clock. But if he came in as a guest with luggage, Sal would have remembered him."

"Do you suppose you can finish these speculations without me?" Dr. Baxter asked. "I'd like to get a little sleep."

"Did you call for the wagon?" Wainwright asked him.

"I'll do it on the way out."

"And what time will you have the autopsy report?"

"When I'm finished!" Baxter snapped, then picked up his bag and strode out.

"Where are his clothes?" Masuto asked.

Again Wainwright looked at Gellman, who shook his head. "We don't know. No sign of them."

Masuto pointed to the dead man's nose. "He wore glasses. There are the marks. Eyeballs enlarged. He was nearsighted, I'd guess. And there's the mark of a watchband on his left wrist. Any sign of the glasses and the wristwatch?"

"No."

Watching Masuto thoughtfully, Wainwright asked, "Anything else, Masao?"

"He wasn't Jewish."

"How the hell—?" Comstock began.

"He's not circumcised, Fred," Gellman explained.

"Go on, Masao."

"Just a few observations that may not mean a thing. He's soft, no sign of physical labor." He picked up one of the dead man's hands. "The nails are cut but not manicured. That's unusual for a guest of his age here in this hotel." He pushed up the man's lip to reveal, among his other teeth, a bridge with a molar of dull gray metal. "I'd guess that isn't

American dental work. He may be a foreigner."

"For God's sake," Gellman said, "I don't want you to try to make something of this, Captain. A man drowned. Let's get the body out of here before the guests wake up, and leave it at that."

"Al, you know better," Wainwright said. "Who is he? Where did he come from? How did he drown—if he did? My word, for a man with his fat to drown in a swimming pool—that's not easy."

"Who discovered the body?" Masuto asked.

Detective Beckman came in at that moment with the day desk clerk, whom Gellman introduced as Ira Jessam. Jessam was forty or so, thin, dark, intense, and very much disturbed by the sight of the dead body.

"Take a good look at him, Mr. Jessam," Wainwright told him, "and tell us whether you ever saw him before."

It was obviously painful for Mr. Jessam to stare at the corpse, more, Masuto suspected, because the man was naked than because he was dead.

Jessam shook his head.

"You never saw him before?"

"He didn't register. That's all I can say. I can't possibly keep track of who goes in and out of the hotel, and anyway there's more than one entrance. But he didn't register while I was on duty."

"All right, Jessam," Gellman said. "Go home and get some sleep. I'll see you tomorrow, or today."

"Not much use in going home now. I think I'll just lie down in the office—if I may."

"Be my guest."

"I'd still like to know who discovered the body," Masuto said.

"Tell him, Beckman," said Wainwright.

"It's the goddamndest thing. According to the night operator, the call came from room three-twenty-two. The room is registered to a guy by the name of Jack Stillman, out of Vegas. He's a booking agent. The call came at exactly two forty-nine, and the operator switched it to the front desk. Now that room overlooks the pool, and the caller tells Frome—he's the night clerk—that there's a body floating in the pool. Frome calls Freddie here"— indicating the security chief—"whose room is on the ground floor off the pool area, and Freddie goes in in his pajamas and drags the fat man out—"

"Which is by no means easy," Comstock observed.

"For God's sake, Freddie," Gellman said, "find a sheet or some towels or something and cover him up." And to Wainwright, "Where the devil's that ambulance? I want him out of here before any of the guests wake up."

"It's coming."

"But now," Beckman said, "we come to the cute part. Both the night operator and the night clerk swear that the call was made by a woman."

"Oh?" Masuto was intrigued.

"Not hysterical. Very cool, very calm. Speaking softly. She talks to the operator first. Then to the front desk."

"What did she say?"

Beckman got out his notebook. "Says to the operator, There's a body floating in the pool. Where, asks the operator? In the swimming pool. The operator says, My God, I'll give you the front desk."

"The operator's a good girl," Gellman said. "Very steady."

"This woman. What did she say to the night clerk?"

"Same thing. Exactly."

"Did he ask who she was?"

"She hung up."

"And room three-twenty-two?"

"I just got down from there when you arrived, Masao. This Stillman guy claims he was asleep. Alone. That's what makes it cute."

"Now look," said Gellman, "this isn't as crazy as it sounds. I know Stillman. He always stays here when he's in L.A. Last month he married Binnie Vance, the dancer. It's his third marriage. All she has to do is find out that he's shacked up with a dame and the shit hits the fan."

"Did you look through his room, bathroom, closets?" Masuto asked.

"What am I, an amateur?"

"Could she slip out of the hotel without being seen?" Masuto asked Gellman.

"I suppose so. Service entrance in the basement. It's bolted on the inside."

He looked at Beckman. "Did you check the bolt?"

"I just got down from the room when you arrived."

"Do it now."

Beckman left. "If she came in her own car," Masuto said, "she wouldn't know where the jockey parked it. If she came with Stillman, she's on foot."

"Where's the phone?" Wainwright demanded.

Gellman pointed to the pool office. A moment later, they heard Wainwright telling the central office to put out a call for any woman on foot. "Give it to L.A.P.D. too," he told them. "She may be a fast walker." He came back as Beckman reappeared.

"The bolt was open," Beckman said.

"I'm going home and get some sleep," said Wainwright. "You take it from here, Masao. And for Christ's sake, if he drowned, he drowned."

"Of course, Captain." Masuto was opening the lockers. "Take that row, Sy," he said to Beckman.

"What the hell are you doing, Masao?"

"He hid his clothes, his glasses and his wristwatch, and then he decided to drown."

"You know what he's after," Gellman sputtered. "He's determined to make something of this. God almighty, a man drowns, he drowns."

"Maybe. Every locker, Sy," Masao said to Beckman.

Gellman turned desperately to Wainwright. "Masao's the boss. It's his case now. I'm going to sleep. Anyway, we won't know how he died until Doc Baxter does the autopsy. Why don't you get some sleep yourself, Al? Good night, gentlemen."

Gellman followed Wainwright out of the dressing room. Masuto and Beckman went through the lockers. The lockers were there for the convenience of the hotel guests, and none of them were locked. The search turned up a number of bathing suits, male, some sunglasses and a wristwatch, all of which Fred Comstock took into his custody. They tried the ladies' dressing room next, and the results were equally uninspiring.

"It's five A.M.," Comstock announced. "I lost a night's sleep, and I don't get overtime, and I'm on duty at eight. How about I sack down for a few hours? You guys don't need me."

"I'll want to talk with Stillman," Masuto said.

"Go ahead. But be gentle. At a hundred dollars a day, they're entitled."

"I'm always gentle."

"The way I figure it," Beckman said, once they were in the elevator, "she made the call while he was sleeping and then skipped."

"You're sure he was asleep?"

"Either that or he was a good actor."

They rang the bell at room 322, and then waited. A second time. Then a third time. Then Jack Stillman opened the door, in his pajamas.

This time he had not been sleeping. The pajamas were heavy black silk, and they had not been slept in. His hair was combed. Stillman was a large, fleshy man, over six feet, with a lot of muscle gone to fat. He had the heavy neck of a football player, cold blue eyes, and brown hair. Behind him, past the small foyer, Masuto saw the unmade bed, an open notebook next to the telephone, and then a window, probably the one that overlooked the pool. The room was overdecorated in the gold and ivory that was a signature for the Beverly Glen Hotel.

"What the hell is this?" Stillman asked unpleasantly.

"I'm Detective Sergeant Masuto, Beverly Hills police. This is Detective Beckman. Are you Stillman?"

"Yes, but it's five o'clock in the morning."

"I'm sorry," Masuto said. "Things happen at inconvenient hours. May we come in?"

"What for?"

"Simply to ask you a few questions."

"He asked questions," indicating Beckman. "I answered them."

"I have some questions of my own."

"Look," said Stillman, "whatever happened here happened when I was asleep. I know nothing, and I don't intend to be pushed around by a couple of small-town cops—not at this hour of the morning."

He started to close the door. Masuto put his shoulder in the way and replied mildly, "Beverly Hills is hardly a small town. We have a population of over thirty thousand, and if you will not talk to us here, Mr. Stillman, we will be happy to wait until you are dressed and then take you downtown, where you can talk to us at the police station."

The cold blue eyes stared at Masuto, and then, unexpectedly, he said, "What are you, Chinese?"

"I am a Nisei, which means that my parents were born in Japan. Now may we come in?"

Beckman recognized the slight hardening in Masuto's voice, very subtle, an indication of closely controlled but increasing anger. Masuto was almost as tall as Stillman, but narrower, leaner, no extra flesh.

Stillman nodded, closing the door behind them. The bedroom was large, with a couch and two brocade armchairs facing the bed, and two windows. The drapes were drawn. Before he sat down, Masuto parted the drapes and looked down at the pool. The first glimmerings of dawn now.

"Sit down," he said to Stillman. Beckman remained standing. Masuto took one chair, Stillman the other.

"The call that informed us that there was the body of a man in the pool came from your room, as Detective Beckman told you earlier," Masuto said.

"It was a mistake. I was asleep from about midnight until he woke me."

"It was not a mistake. A woman made the call. Mr. Stillman, a woman used the telephone in this room. I want to know who she was."

"I told you—"

"Would it be easier," Masuto interrupted, "if I gave the story to the Los Angeles *Times*, specifying that a nameless woman who shared this room with you discovered a body in the swimming pool in the middle of the night?"

"Who the hell—"

Again Masuto interrupted. "Suppose you just tell us what happened and stop the indignation."

"What then? Do you still give it to the papers?"

"Only if I must. Possibly not. I'm not a reporter, I'm a policeman."

"All right. Look, understand me. I don't give a damn about my reputation. I live in Vegas, and nobody's going to fault me for wanting my bed warm. But I was just married to Binnie Vance, and she'll cut my heart out if she hears about this. I picked up this dame in the Rugby Room, and I bought her a drink, and then I bought her dinner. She was a pro. I paid fifty bucks for last night, but like I said, she was a pro, and she didn't rip off my wallet when she left. I respect that. I respect integrity in any line of work. That's the whole story. If she made the call, she made it without waking me. I was asleep. I didn't lie about that."

"I'm glad you have principles," Masuto said.

"What the hell does that mean?"

"What was her name?"

"Judy."

"Judy what?"

"I don't know."

"You went to bed with a woman and you don't know her last name?"

"Jesus Christ, I didn't marry the broad. She tells me her name was Judy. I didn't ask for her birth certificate."

"What does she look like?"

"Not like a hooker." Stillman was trying to be helpful. "You get a classy kind of broad in the Rugby Room, five seven, stacked, blond hair, blue eyes—a good-looking kid."

Beckman was taking it down in his pad. "What was she wearing?"

"Let's see—silk shirt, tan suede pants, same color, or almost, boots—"

"Boots?"

"Boots."

"What kind of jacket?"

"Same thing as the pants, suede. Four gold chains around her neck."

Out in the hall, Beckman said to Masuto, "Where does it get us? So she saw fatso in the pool and reported it. Another dame would have kept her mouth shut."

"That makes Judy a little special, doesn't it?"

"For a hooker."

"For a person."

"What now?"

"Take a look around the basement before you leave, Sy—laundry bins, that kind of thing. See if you can dig up his clothes."

"And you?"

"I'll phone in the description, and then I'm going home for a hot bath."

"And what about me?"

"What about you?"

"Do I get to sleep?"

"Tonight."

"It is tonight," Beckman said.

"Not anymore. It's tomorrow."

2

THE
SHOT
MAN

Masuto lay steaming luxuriously in water as hot as he could bear. Kati, having just seen the children into their school bus, entered the bathroom with an enormous white towel and settled herself on the stool to await her husband's completion of his bath. To Masuto, a hot bath was not simply a hot bath; it was the continuation of an ancient ritual without which life would have been considerably less tolerable.

He had already told her about the incidents of the night, and now she said, rather plaintively, "You know that I have never been to the Beverly Glen Hotel. Wouldn't it be pleasant if we could have dinner there some night and I could see that famous Rugby Room? My mother would be happy to stay with the children."

"No."

"But she would."

"I was not referring to your excellent mother, but to the Beverly Glen Hotel."

"But why?"

"Kati, darling, I dislike being judgmental about the City of Beverly Hills, since they pay me my wages. The hotel is another matter. It makes my skin crawl."

"But why?"

Masuto sighed and shook his head. "How can I explain why? Perhaps another time. Hand me the towel, please."

He meditated for half an hour before he left the house, sitting cross-legged, wrapped in a saffron-colored robe, silent and motionless until his mind was clear and alert. When he had finished he felt renewed and refreshed, and on his way to Rexford Drive, where police headquarters was, he thought a good deal about the drowned man. It promised to be a quiet day—so far, at nine-thirty, no robberies, no assaults, nothing of importance on his desk except an inquiry from the city manager concerning the drowned man.

"What about the media?" Masuto asked Beckman.

"I'm sitting on it until I hear from Wainwright. He's not in yet."

"How does Joe Haley know about it?" Haley was the city manager.

"I told him."

"What?"

"Just that there was a drowning."

"That's no good. Go up there and give him the whole story, the missing clothes, everything. I don't want him to scream about us covering up anything. Let him decide whether he wants to keep a lid on it. Did you hear from Doc Baxter?"

"I called his home just before you came in. He's on his way to the hospital."

"You didn't find his clothes?" Masuto asked, almost as an afterthought.

"No."

"Okay. If Wainwright wants me, tell him I'm at the hospital—down in the pathology room."

Beckman looked at him curiously. "Are you on to something, Masao?"

"I don't like a drowned man who undresses himself and then hides his own clothes. Do you?"

Driving to the hospital, Masuto wondered whether he was unduly harsh with Beckman. Sy Beckman was a large, lumbering, slow-moving man, not stupid, but slow in his conclusions, and totally dependable. Given his choice, Masuto would rather have Beckman than any other man on the force. Yet there were times when Beckman irritated him, and reflecting on that now, he determined to go out of his way to be pleasant, even grateful. He felt better then. It was a lovely morning, and his car radio told him that there would be a minimum of smog. Well, that at least was something, not great but better than those hideous days when the Los Angeles basin filled up with the noxious yellow stuff. Masuto had been born in the San Fernando Valley, in the long, long ago when his father owned a four-acre produce farm outside of what was then the little village of San Fernando—a farm that he lost when he was interned during the madness of World War II. Then the Valley had been like a garden, and no one ever thought about a thing called smog. Ah well, that was long ago and over now. Los Angeles was still for him the best of all possible places.

At the hospital, he showed his badge to the clerk at the pathology room and then went inside—trying not to breathe too deeply of the smell of formaldehyde, which he disliked intensely—past three young, bearded men who were bent over microscopes, to the autopsy room, where Dr. Baxter was leaning over the corpse of the drowned man.

Baxter straightened up, saw Masuto, and said graciously, "What the hell are you doing here?"

"Just curious."

"You're not a policeman, you're a damn ghoul. You just can't stand a natural death."

"I don't enjoy any kind of death," Masuto replied gently. "Was his death natural?"

"He drowned. That's natural enough for someone who can't swim and takes a few too many."

"Mostly, people who can't swim don't go swimming."

"I'm tired, Masuto. I'm in no mood for Oriental philosophy."

"If that's philosophy, heaven help us. Are you sure he died of drowning?"

"You're damn right I'm sure. Water in the lungs—all of it. He drowned. No marks, no sign of violence."

"How many drinks? Was he drunk?"

"No, he was not drunk—unless two or three drinks wiped him out."

"Then why did he drown?"

"Because he couldn't swim. Why don't you leave it alone?"

"I suppose because both Gellman and you want me to.

That brings out the nastiness in my nature. Have you spoken to Gellman today?"

"That's none of your damn business, Masuto."

"You're the attending physician up there at the hotel. You're also the medical examiner for the city."

"What are you insinuating?"

"Nothing so awful. Gellman wants it to be an accident. I refuse to accept the fact that a fat man who would float like a cork makes his clothes, his watch, and his spectacles disappear and then proceeds to drown himself in a swimming pool. The pool is only sixty feet long. From the shallow end there's twenty-five feet before it deepens to five feet. Did he suffer a coronary? Did he have angina?"

Baxter hesitated. "No."

"Then he was poisoned, which means he was murdered."

"There's no sign of poisoning."

"What about the contents of his stomach?"

"I haven't gotten to that."

"And if you find nothing," Masuto insisted, "I still say he was poisoned."

"By what? By the smog?" Baxter asked sarcastically.

"I suggest chloral hydrate, more commonly known as a Mickey Finn. You'd find no trace of that, no matter how you tested. And how do you know he had only two or three drinks? Did you test for alcohol in his blood?"

"Damn you, Masuto, don't tell me how to do my job."

"Then don't tell me how to do mine," Masuto said, smiling slightly. "By the way, when you're finished, put him in the icebox. I want him to stay fresh for identification."

"Your photographer was here and he took pictures."

"I know. Please forgive my insistence. I think whoever

comes looking for him will want to see him in the flesh."

"He won't keep forever."

"A few days will do."

Masuto pulled back the man's upper lip and stared thoughtfully.

"You are a ghoul," Baxter said.

"And I would deeply appreciate a telephone call, concerning whatever you find in his stomach or in his blood."

Baxter grunted. Masuto thanked him and got out of the pathology room and breathed deeply outside. Back in his office, he still had the illusion of smelling the formaldehyde. He hated the smell.

"That's one place I do not like," Detective Beckman said, after Masuto told him what had taken place. "Anyway, Masao, what makes you think that you can't detect chloral hydrate in an autopsy?"

"Something I read somewhere."

"You talk about the stink of formaldehyde. The same thing for chloral hydrate. It stinks."

"In a drink?"

"Well, maybe a few drops in a drink couldn't be smelled. You think the fat man got a Mickey and drowned?"

"Something of the sort."

Masuto picked up the telephone and dialed Dr. Rosenberg, his dentist. Beckman drifted away, yawning. Dr. Rosenberg came on the phone.

"You're due for a cleaning, Masao. We sent you two notices. None of you turkeys understand the necessity for prophylactic dentistry. It's like shouting in the wilderness."

"Next week," Masuto promised.

"So you say. I'm putting my nurse on. Make a date with her."

"Hold on. I have a question."

"Oh?"

"Did you ever see a false tooth or a cap or a bridge or something like that made out of some grayish metal?"

"Silver?"

"I don't think silver. Maybe an aluminum alloy, maybe steel."

"I've seen it," Dr. Rosenberg said, his tone indicating severe disapproval.

"Where? When?"

"Russian dentistry, if you call it dentistry. They wouldn't use gold. Too expensive or bourgeois, and they just weren't any good with ceramics. Back during the war, we liberated a batch of Russian prisoners and I saw a lot of it, aluminum alloy and even steel—lousy dentistry. I don't know if they still do it."

"Thanks, Dave—"

"Hold on. I'll put on the nurse."

Masuto made his appointment for a prophylactic treatment, and Beckman, still yawning, drifted back and sat down opposite him. "Don't you want to know what Joe Haley had to say?"

"I do."

"Nothing."

"Nothing?"

"Not exactly nothing. He said that keeping the reputation of Beverly Hills clean is like trying to canonize Marie Duplessis. Who is Marie Duplessis?"

"The most notorious hooker of nineteenth-century Paris.

Sy, let me ask you a few questions. First. Stillman says he picked up this girl, Judy, in the Rugby Room. How did she get there?"

"How does anyone get there?"

"Exactly. By car. No one walks to the Beverly Glen Hotel. It's not on the street. It's on a hill and there's not even a sidewalk."

"So she drove."

"But nobody saw her. And if she cut out of there by the basement door, what happened to her car?"

"That's an interesting question," Beckman admitted.

"Next. Why the missing clothes?"

"That one's easy, Masao. They don't want the body identified."

"But sooner or later, it will be, so we can conclude that they're playing for time. Next question."

Wainwright walked into the office in time to hear that, and asked whether they were playing guessing games or just killing time.

"That's right. Next question. A woman sees a body in a swimming pool. She doesn't get excited or hysterical, just calls the operator and tells her. Why?"

"You tell us," said Wainwright.

"Because she knows he's dead; because she killed him."

"Goddamn it, Masao, you can't operate like that. You don't know if the man was murdered, and already you got a killer."

The telephone rang, and Beckman answered it. "Yeah," he said. "Yeah. Okay. Yeah."

"That was Baxter, Captain."

"Oh?"

"He said he thinks he found traces of chloral hydrate in the fat man's stomach. He can't be sure, but he thinks so. He doesn't like you," he said to Masuto.

"So sorry. So we have a murder. What about the alcohol?"

"The man was drunk—maybe," Beckman said.

"A little drunk, perhaps. High. He strips and goes into the pool, falls asleep and drowns."

"The trouble is," Wainwright said, "that when you come down to it, we're a small town with a small-town police force, and still we got a collection of some of the most important characters in the country, and if they don't live here, then they come here. This one bothers me."

Masuto nodded. "That's understandable. I think he's a Russian."

"Why?"

"Just a guess. My dentist, Dr. Rosenberg, suggests that his bridgework comes from there."

"Gellman's going to love that. A dead Russian in the Beverly Glen pool." Wainwright turned to Beckman. "Put his picture on the wire to Washington. We'll see if the F.B.I. can come up with something."

Masuto picked up the telephone, dialed Information, and asked for the telephone number of the Soviet consul general. He listened for a moment, thanked the operator and put down the phone.

"What are you after, Masuto?" Wainwright wanted to know.

"Just fishing. Did you know the Russians don't have a consulate here? The operator thinks they have one in San Francisco." Beckman was coming back. Masuto called, "Sy, find a San Francisco phone book, and give me the L.A. *Times*—today, yesterday, the day before."

"And goddamn it, stop yawning!" Wainwright snapped.

Wainwright watched with interest as Masuto dialed the San Francisco number and asked for the consul general. Then Masuto said, "No, I insist on speaking to him. This is an official call from the Beverly Hills police on a matter of the utmost importance." Pause. "Yes, Detective Sergeant Masuto." Pause. "Yes, I'll wait."

Masuto looked at Wainwright, who nodded, apparently intrigued. Then Masuto covered the phone and told Beckman, "Start going through the papers. Anything that concerns Russia and Los Angeles, any connection."

Beckman spread out the papers. Masuto spoke into the phone: "How do you do, sir. I am Detective Sergeant Masuto in Beverly Hills. We have an unexplained death, a drowning—" Pause. "No, sir. This is your business and it does concern you. I have some reason to believe that the dead man is a Russian national." Pause. "About fifty-five years old, thin blond hair, five feet eight inches, blue eyes—" Pause. "No, sir. I did not say that he is thin. His hair is thin. He's a fat man, quite fat." Pause. "No, sir, there is no way we can identify him. He was found naked, drowned in the pool." Pause. "Yes, sir, I understand. We will do our best, but I cannot promise." Pause. "Yes, the police station is on Rexford Drive in Beverly Hills. Any cab driver."

Masuto put down the phone and looked at Wainwright. "Well?"

"The Soviet consul general will be on the first shuttle flight he can catch. He will be here today, early afternoon."

The telephone rang, and Masuto picked it up. "Yes," he

said. "This is Detective Sergeant Masuto." Pause. "Yes, I just spoke to the consul general. I understand."

"Checking," Wainwright said.

"They're thorough."

"What can't you promise?"

"Like Mr. Gellman," Masuto said, "he wants it kept out of the press."

"Masao?" Beckman said.

"Find something?"

"Just this, and I don't know if it means a goddamn thing."

Wainwright took the paper from Beckman and read aloud, "Mayor Bradley was on hand to extend an official welcome to five Soviet agronomists, here on a three-day visit to observe orange growing in Los Angeles and Orange counties. From here, they will fly to Florida, for an extended seven-day tour of the Florida orange groves—" Wainwright paused and stared at Masuto. "What do we have, a dead agronomist?"

"What the hell is an agronomist?" Beckman wanted to know.

"An educated farmer," Masuto said. "No—" He closed his eyes and shook his head. "No, I don't think we have a dead agronomist."

"Why not?"

Masuto shrugged. "Nearsighted, fat, soft hands—it just doesn't fit. Anyway—" He picked up the paper and scanned the story. "You see, they move in a group. If one were missing—no." He stood up suddenly and said, "I'm going to the hotel. Sy, see if you can catch up with the agronomists."

"And do what?"

"I don't know. Nose around."

"Nose around," Wainwright said sourly. "I'm not running a police force. I'm running a goddamn curiosity shop. Masao, I want you back here when that Russian comes." He started away, then turned back. "I'll talk to L.A.P.D. and see what they're doing with these Russian farmers. Now I got your disease."

Sal Monti, doorman at the Beverly Glen Hotel, was reputed to have a very large income, even in a city of noticeably large incomes, even after his split with the hotel management. He ran a service with four assistant carhops, and having seen the way traffic poured into the hotel driveway around lunchtime and cocktail hour, Masuto felt that Monti was understaffed. He was skilled in what he did, had a remarkable memory, and had held down his post for the past dozen years, a long history in the life of Beverly Hills—measured, as Monti put it, from the time of the T-Bird, through the Lincoln Continental period, through the era of the large Cadillac, through the era of the Porsche, into the time of the Mercedes, which shared the present reign with the Seville. It was Monti who coined the phrase "Beverly Hills Volkswagen" for the Mercedes. The present era, just burgeoning, was that of the Rolls-Royce Corniche; and at every opportunity, Monti told the story of the film producer who bought a solid silver funeral casket for sixty thousand dollars and whose partner remarked, as Monti put it, "Shmuck, for the same money you could have been buried in a Corniche." Now he eyed Masuto's Toyota with tolerant disgust.

"Sergeant," he said, "there is going to be a house rule against economy cars. It cuts the ambiance, if you know what I mean."

"I'll look it up in the dictionary," Masuto said. "Meanwhile, I want a few minutes of your time."

"About the excitement last night? By all means. You can fill me in."

"No, Sal. You fill me in."

"It's eleven-fifteen," Monti observed. "We got forty-five minutes before the rush starts. Billy," he called to one of the carhops, "take over." They sat down on an iron bench under the striped canopy that led into the hotel.

"Tell me about Jack Stillman," Masuto began.

"This fat guy—what is it? Was he knocked over or what?"

"I'll ask the questions. Tell me about Stillman."

"What's to tell? He's a booking agent out of Vegas—so it goes. He stayed here maybe half a dozen times."

"What does he book?"

"I'd give it a guess. The high-priced acts in the casinos. He just married Binnie Vance, the exotic dancer. She's very hot right now. Or maybe he don't book at all. Who knows with them characters from Vegas?"

"And when he's here, do you see him with girls?"

"I guess he was a swinger, as much as the next guy. Not on this trip."

"You're sure?"

"I'm only sure about what goes in and out of this place. What happens inside is another department. Are you going to give me some flak about the fat man?"

"What are they saying?"

"Nothing. Gellman's put the fear of God into them. I got it from Freddie Comstock, and he don't say one word more than that they had a drowning."

"Sal," Masuto said, "how many hookers work the Rugby Room?"

"Are you kidding! Sarge, this is a high-class hotel. We got an international reputation. We got presidents and senators going in and out of here. That's no question to ask. You know that."

"Cut out the bullshit, Sal. How many? It's important."

"Well, look. You don't get floozies or streetwalkers in a place like this. It's a different kind of a hustle. A girl works in the Rugby Room, she don't look no different from the classy broads you see on the street in Beverly Hills. Maybe she ain't no different. They got class, good clothes, rocks, and they got the looks. They make out for fifty to two notes for a quick throw, and that don't include dinner and drinks. We don't have no pimps here, Sarge, you know that. It's a whole other thing. They come in by twos, two girls, because Fritz won't seat one broad alone in the Rugby Room—"

"They buy the ticket from you, Sal," Masuto said coldly. "Either you talk sense to me, or I'll bust your whole operation wide open."

"Sarge, you got to be kidding. All right, a man works the door, he depends on tips."

"I asked you how many?"

"Okay, okay. Maybe a dozen. Then there are floaters. They drive up in a two-seater Mercedes, in a twenty-five-thousand-dollar car—what am I supposed to do? Be a vice squad?"

"Begin with the dozen regulars. I'm looking for a woman named Judy, about five seven, good figure, blond hair, blue eyes."

"That ain't no description, Sarge. That's like a uniform. Anyway, in what you call the regulars there ain't nobody called Judy."

"She was wearing a pants suit, light brown suede, silk

shirt, gold chains, those boots they wear now."

Monti shood his head. "It don't register."

"Did anyone fitting that description drive up to the hotel last night?"

"Blue eyes, blond hair, stacked—you just got to be kidding. I can name you twenty."

"And the costume?"

Sal frowned and shook his head. "Jesus, Sarge, when the rush comes, I see them, I write the tickets, but the clothes. Maybe yes, maybe no."

"How about this morning? Forget about the clothes. Did anyone fitting the description come out of the hotel?"

Monti pointed to the door of the hotel. "Sarge, just watch that door, and if five minutes goes by without a blue-eyed blond broad going in or out, I'll cut you into my take. It all comes out of the same bottle. It's the Beverly Hills color. If they want blue eyes, they buy tinted contact lenses. If they want to be stacked, they buy that too. You know that as well as I do."

Masuto sighed and nodded. "All right, Sal. Thank you." He rose. "One more thing—did you see Stillman this morning?"

"Not yet, Sarge."

"You'd know if he called for his car?"

"You bet."

"What does he drive?"

"He picks up a rental at the airport, usually a caddy. A yellow one this time."

"Look in your box for the keys."

Monti went to the key box, opened it, and stared at the rows of hooks. Then he looked at Masuto. Then he yelled,

"Billy, run down the hill and see if Stillman's yellow caddy is still there!"

Billy took off down the hill. Monti went through the motions with the people entering and leaving the hotel, and Masuto waited in silence. Then Billy came pounding back up the hill.

"The caddy's gone."

"You made a note of the license?" Masuto asked Monti.

Monti went through his cards. "Here it is." Masuto jotted it down, Monti telling him meanwhile that there was no way—just no way the keys could have gotten out of his box.

"Except the way they did. Do you lock the box?"

"Hell, no. It's right here."

Masuto went into the hotel and walked over to the registration desk. Ira Jessam, the day clerk, looked at him sadly and said, "That was a terrible thing last night, Sergeant, just terrible."

Masuto agreed and asked him to ring Stillman's room. The desk clerk picked up his phone, gave his instructions to the operator and waited.

"Mr. Stillman doesn't answer," he said.

"Does he drop his keys at the desk when he leaves the hotel?"

"Always."

"Are they there now?"

The clerk looked. "No, sir. But he could be in the restaurant."

"Call them."

The clerk did so, and then put down his phone and shook his head.

"I'd like a duplicate key to his room," Masuto said.

Jessam hesitated, then sighed and handed the key to Masuto, who asked him where Gellman was.

"In his office, I believe. Probably taking a nap. He was utterly exhausted."

"Wake him up and tell him I'm going up to Stillman's room. I'd like him to join me there."

Masuto took the elevator up to the third floor. The chambermaid's cart was in the hallway, and several room doors were open. On the door of Stillman's room there was a "Do not disturb" sign. Masuto put his key in the lock and opened the door.

The bed was unmade. In one corner, Stillman's underwear, shirt and socks, lying in a little pile. Masuto had noticed them the day before. The bathroom door was closed, and from behind it came the sound of running water. The windows were closed and the air in the room smelled stale. On the chest of drawers, a bottle of brandy and two glasses. The ashtrays were filled with half-smoked cigarettes, most of them impatiently crushed out.

Closing the door behind him, Masuto called out, "Stillman!" No response from the bathroom. He tapped on the bathroom door and repeated Stillman's name. Then he opened the door.

The water in the sink was running. On the floor in front of the sink was Stillman, in his black pajamas. Masuto bent over him and felt for his pulse. His wrist was cold; as for his pulse, he had none. Then Masuto noticed a small spot of blood in Stillman's hair on the back of his head. He moved the hair aside, and there was a bullet hole where his spine joined the back of his skull. He lay with his face against the floor, and Masuto did not touch him again or try to move him. Using his handkerchief, Masuto turned off the faucet. It was the hot water faucet. Stillman evidently had been shaving. The razor lay on the floor beside him. A tube of shaving cream was on the sink shelf, and by bending over the body, Masuto could see that much of his face was still lathered.

Masuto went back into the bedroom, picked up the telephone, and dialed his headquarters. "Joyce," he said to the operator, "this is Masuto. Give me Captain Wainwright."

"Masao," Wainwright said, "where the hell are you? It's almost twelve, and I want you here when that Russian shows up. And by the way, the F.B.I. knows who our drowned man is. I didn't think those jokers knew which side was up, but they pegged him right off. And it's got class, Masao. They asked me not to pass it on to the local clowns. They're flying some special character in from Washington—his name is Arvin Clinton, but that's between you and me. Nothing to anyone else, nothing to the papers. This is a doozy. Nobody wants publicity. So just get your ass over here."

"That's all very interesting," Masuto agreed.

"Thank you. Did you hear me? Where the devil are you?"

"At the hotel."

"Good. Nothing to Gellman. Just tell him that we'll cooperate to keep a lid on this if he'll just bottle up the loudmouths at the hotel."

"I'm in Jack Stillman's room."

"Christ, he couldn't listen in?"

"No, Captain. He's dead."

"What!"

"Someone shot him through the back of the head while he was shaving."

"You're putting me on."

"I'm afraid not."

"Dead?"

"Dead."

"Murdered?"

"It would seem so. The back of his head and no gun in sight."

"Anyone else there?"

"Just me. I thought I'd talk to him again. I waited too long."

"Gellman will truly have a fit when he hears about this."

"I think I hear him knocking at the door," Masuto said. "I told him to meet me here."

"All right. Keep him there until I get there. I'll call Baxter and have him meet us there. Christ, Masao, what about the Russian?"

"He can't get to L.A. before another hour. No way. I have to answer the door."

Masuto hung up the telephone and went to the door.

3

THE
SOVIET
MAN

Masuto opened the door, and Gellman slipped into the room, closing the door behind him.

"Are you alone?" he whispered.

Masuto nodded.

His voice rose. "Masao, you are putting me in one hell of a position. It's not enough that I got a drowning on my hands and the owners are threatening me and my wife thinks I'm shacking up here and I haven't slept in two days, but on top of all that you got to search a guest's room. Jessam ought to be fired for giving you the key. You can't do it. Do you have a warrant?" he asked as an afterthought.

Masuto shook his head.

"Then you're out of your mind. It's a violation. You know that. If Stillman finds out, he could sue us to hell."

"He won't find out."

"How do you know? He could walk in right now."

"I wish he could, but he can't," Masuto said gently. "He's dead."

"He is what?"

"Dead. He's lying in the bathroom with a bullet in his head."

"No. No. Look," Gellman said, his hand trembling, "I got ulcers and before this is over I'm going to have a coronary to go with it. So cut out the gags."

"Sit down," Masuto said, pointing to a chair. "Sit down and pull yourself together."

Gellman collapsed into a chair. "Do you know what this is going to do to the hotel?"

"It's even worse for Stillman. It happened. Now take it easy. I'm going to call Fred Comstock. Is he in his office?"

Gellman nodded, got to his feet and started to reach for the brandy bottle on top of the chest of drawers.

"Don't touch anything!" Masuto snapped at him. "Just sit down and pull yourself together." He picked up the phone, dialed the operator, and asked for Comstock.

"I got to see what's in that bathroom," Gellman said weakly.

"First pull yourself together." Into the phone, "Fred, this is Masuto. I'm in room three-twenty-two with Gellman. Get up here. It's important."

"He had to kill himself," Gellman moaned. "That inconsiderate son of a bitch! Masao, suicide is the god-damned most inconsiderate thing a person can do. They never think of anyone but themselves."

"He didn't kill himself, Al. He was murdered."

"Murdered?"

"That's right. Someone shot him in the back of the head."

"Oh, God. I thought it was bad, but this—"

"You might as well know, Al, the fat man was also murdered."

"They said he was drowned."

"Drugged and then drowned."

"Oh, brother, this is one stinking nightmare. Masao, for God's sake, can we keep a lid on this?"

"Maybe on the fat man, Al. There's a whole committee that wants to keep a lid on that one. But this? No. There's no way."

The doorbell rang. Masuto went to the door and Comstock came in.

"If it takes money," Gellman was saying, "we can pay. I'll talk to the city manager. I know the Chandlers—"

"What in hell is going on in here?" Comstock wanted to know. "This is Stillman's room. Where is he?"

"He's lying in the bathroom, dead, bullet in the back of his head. Mr. Gellman's disturbed, naturally." Comstock's mouth fell. He looked from Gellman to Masuto, who went on, "Captain Wainwright's on his way over, and he'll have Sy Beckman with him and Sweeney, the fingerprint man, and the photographer and maybe a uniformed cop or two. Then Doc Baxter will be coming, and he's got a loud mouth. Then the ambulance will be here to take the body away. Now what we don't want, Fred, is to make this any worse for Al than it already is, so go down to the front and talk to Sal Monti, and tell him to ease everyone in with no questions. If a black-and-white comes, have it pull down the row and park with no commotion. Just try to keep it going very quiet and easy, and tell the people downstairs to keep their peace and not to talk."

"Where is he? The stiff?"

"Quiet and easy," Gellman said. "Right in the lunch hour. There'll be fifty cars into the hotel in the next half hour."

"In the bathroom, I told you," Masuto said to Comstock, who started for the bathroom door. "Leave it alone, Fred. I don't want anything touched. Now please, go down and do what I told you to."

He hesitated, and Gellman said weakly, "Go ahead, Fred. Do what Masao told you to. He knows what he's doing."

Comstock grunted and left the room.

"I wish I did," Masuto said. He closed his eyes and stood silently in the center of the room.

"What the devil are you doing?"

"Trying to think some sense into this."

"Can we open a window? I'm choking."

Masuto went over to the manager and patted him softly on the shoulder. "Not yet. I want to leave everything just as it is until Sweeney gets here. I don't believe you solve anything with fingerprints, but that's his stock in trade, and he's touchy about it. Try to relax. Tell me, Al, when do you open the pool in the morning for the guests?"

"At nine o'clock."

"Did you open it this morning?"

He nodded.

"Who does it?"

"Joe Finnuchi, the pool man. He has a kid who assists him, a college kid who works as pool boy during the summer. His name is Bobby Carlton."

"When they open in the morning, is anyone there waiting to use the pool?"

"Yeah, there's always three or four health nuts down for their morning swim. Sometimes more. I don't know what you're getting at, Masao. What difference does it make?"

"Maybe none. I'm just trying to understand that public-spirited prostitute who called in the information about the drowned man in the middle of the night. The point is, Al, that if she'd left it alone and this Joe Finnuchi and the pool boy and the guests had walked into the pool area, the news of the drowned man would be all over the hotel and the city and the country too."

"So we lucked out—until this."

"No. She was just buying time. But why? That's why he was naked. Eight hours, and we still don't know who he is. Why did she need the eight hours?"

"What are you talking about?"

"Al, listen to me. The fat man's clothes are somewhere in the hotel. I want them. Will you give it a try?"

"How do you know?"

"Just accept the fact that I know. Will you tell Comstock to really shake down the place—every place someone in a hurry might hide clothes, shoes, and the rest of it?"

"Two murders, and you tell me to shake down the place and find the clothes of a man who wasn't even a guest here, and he has to go and pick this place to get himself murdered."

The doorbell rang, and Masuto opened it for Wainwright, Sweeney, Beckman, Haskins, the police photographer, and trailing them, Doc Baxter, whose sour glance at Masuto indicated that the detective was solely responsible for dragging him over here.

"I do hope to hell you haven't loused everything up," Sweeney said by way of introduction.

"We haven't touched a thing."

"Where is he?" Baxter demanded.

Masuto led them to the bathroom. "Use your hand-kerchief!" Sweeney yelled as he reached for the door. Masuto nodded, did as he was told, and opened the door. Baxter bent over Stillman's body.

"He's dead," he told them.

"I thought so," Masuto said.

"Don't give me your smartass talk. He's dead when I say so. One shot at the base of the skull, very effective and quick. Close range—see where the hair is singed."

"Small gun, small caliber," Masuto said, almost apolo-getically. "Small enough to fit in the palm of her hand. She just reached up and fired the bullet into the back of his head."

"She? She? What the hell do you mean, Masao?"

"He was shaving, Captain. He was looking into the mirror. So he saw whoever came into the bathroom, and apparently he didn't even turn around. Someone he knew. If it were a man, he would have seen the movement of his hands in the mirror. The movements of a small woman would be entirely concealed behind his back. She could snuggle up to him, and then just slide the gun up and kill him."

"You're telling me that some dame could be cold-blooded enough—"

"It's happened. We underestimate women."

"How long ago?" Wainwright asked Baxter.

"Maybe three or four hours," flexing Stillman's fingers. "Maybe eight o'clock this morning, maybe nine." He straightened up and picked up his bag. "Well, that's that. You don't need me here anymore. Never needed me in the first place. I'll poke around at the hospital and have the reports filled in. I want a card with his name tied to his hand. I'm rotten with names." And with that he bustled out through the door, sending a last nasty glance at Masuto.

"He's a sweetheart," Beckman said.

"Stay with Sweeney," Wainwright said to Beckman. "Once he's lifted his prints, I want every corner of this place turned inside out." And to Sweeney, "I want a full set of Stillman's prints before they take him away, and when you get back to the office, put them on the wire to Washington and give them to L.A.P.D. as well. Nobody just gets himself shot. There's got to be some sanity in this."

"In murder?" Masuto said. "There never is, you know."

Gellman said, "Look, Captain—I'm destroyed, so I'm not asking for pity. But if you have that body carried through the hotel—how do you do it?"

"The ambulance is on its way."

"You mean the morgue wagon?"

"Al, get hold of yourself. We don't have a morgue wagon. We got an arrangement with All Saints Hospital, and we use their pathology room and morgue. So it will just be an ambulance and some interns in white coats or whatever. It's done, and life goes on."

"Fool, fool!" Masuto exclaimed, and reached for the phone.

"Handkerchief!" Sweeney yelled.

Masuto dialed headquarters while the others watched curiously. He told Joyce, the operator, "I want an All Points Bulletin on a yellow Cadillac. First check all the car rentals at the airport and find out what kind of car Jack Stillman of Las Vegas rented. No. No, forget that. I have the license number." He fumbled through his pockets, found the slip.

"Here it is, seven-six-nine-two VVN, give it to everyone, our own cars, L.A.P.D., the sheriff, the Highway Patrol. High priority. Possibly driven by a woman. Even if it is a woman, she is armed and dangerous. I want the car located and anyone in it held for questioning."

He put down the phone and turned to face Wainwright. "I should have thought of it immediately." He shrugged. "Well, it's three or four hours since Stillman died, so I don't suppose it matters, They'll probably find the car parked somewhere."

"What the devil is this all about?" Wainwright demanded.

Masuto looked at his watch. "Twelve-thirty," he said to Wainwright. "We ought to get back before the Russian comes."

Wainwright started to say something, swallowed, and said to Beckman, "Sit on this, Sy." And to Gellman, "When Sweeney's finished, Al, we'll have to close up the room. At least for twenty-four hours."

"With a cop outside?" Gellman asked plaintively.

"Okay, I'll tell the cop to go."

"And what do I do now?"

"You'll have the press all over you. They'll keep you busy."

"What do I tell them?"

"About the drowned man—if they ask, just tell them that he drowned. If they don't ask, tell them nothing. About Stillman, he's a guy from Vegas and he got shot. It happens."

"He's not just a guy from Vegas. He's Binnie Vance's husband and manager."

"Who the hell is Binnie Vance?"

"You don't live right, Captain," Sweeney said, pausing in his dusting. "Binnie Vance is only the hottest thing that hit Vegas this season. She's an exotic dancer who makes Gypsy Rose Lee look like a Girl Scout entertainer."

"Gypsy Rose Lee—you got to be kidding. That goes back thirty years."

"So do I," said Sweeney.

"Well, whoever she is, she's got to be told that Stillman is dead. Where do you suppose she is?"

"Probably in Las Vegas," Beckman said.

"Oh, great, great," Gellman said. "Do you know what the goddamn media is going to do? They're going to make it a mob execution."

"I told you a woman killed him," Masuto said. "The mob doesn't have women executioners, not yet."

In the hallway, Wainwright told the uniformed policeman that he could go back to his car, and then he said to Masuto, "You seem damned sure that a woman did it."

"Not positive. I think so."

"And you also know who she is," Wainwright observed sarcastically.

"I think so. But that doesn't mean one damn thing, Captain. It's just a wild guess, and I don't know why or how it adds up or comes together or what it all means."

"And you also know who killed the fat man?"

"Sort of."

They were in the elevator now, along with the uniformed cop and two hotel guests, so Wainwright held his peace. But when they got out into the lobby, Wainwright snapped, "What the hell do you mean, sort of? Even from you, that's a new one."

"Captain, look at that," the uniformed officer said,

pointing to Sal Monti, talking to half a dozen reporters and cameramen.

"That little son of a bitch," Wainwright snorted. "Where's your car, Masao? You got the keys or did you give them to Monti?"

"I'm down the hill and I have the keys."

"Good. I came with Beckman, so you drive. We go right through. Not one word."

They were past the entrance before someone recognized Wainwright, and then the reporters raced after the captain and Masuto. "Nothing!" Wainwright snapped at them. "Not one word! Not one comment! Go back and talk to Gellman."

When they were in the car, Masuto said gently, "You could have given them something."

"No, sir. Not one word out of either of us. This is tangled up with Washington, and nobody says that you or me shot our mouths off. Now what the hell is all this about knowing who did it?"

"I don't know, I make guesses. What is a guess worth when you don't have motive or a shred of evidence?"

"You wouldn't like to tell me?"

"To what end? Your guess is as good as mine."

"Like hell it is. I don't know why I put up with you, Masao. You are the most peculiar Oriental son of a bitch I ever encountered. Now what the devil is all this about a yellow caddy and the All Points?"

"Stillman rented the yellow Cadillac at the airport. Someone took the keys out of Monti's box this morning and drove it away."

"You said a woman."

"That was a guess. I think a woman killed Stillman. I

think the same woman drove off in his car. Nothing's going to come of that, believe me, Captain. You said the F.B.I. knows who the dead man is. Who is he?"

"I never liked that little bastard."

"What little bastard?"

"Sal Monti. Someone just takes the keys out of his box. Horseshit."

"It can happen. What about the fat man?"

"This is what I got from the F.B.I. I told you they're sending a special man out here. I hate those bastards. I guess every cop in America hates them. Anyway, according to the Feds, the dead man's name is Peter Litovsky. He's attached to the Soviet embassy in Washington as cultural attaché, whatever that means."

"It's a very minor post. I imagine his job would be to effect cultural exchanges, keep us posted on what is happening in the Russian theater, concert stage, and so on. And the same thing in the other direction."

"That may be, except that this Litovsky is not what he seems to be. The Feds say that he's one of the top men in Soviet Intelligence, whatever their equivalent of the C.I.A. is, and that he uses the cultural attaché job as a cover, and what I can't understand is that if they know all this, why in hell do they let him operate?"

"I suppose because we do the same thing."

"And instead of being pleased that he's dead, they're in a lather over it. Goddamn it, Masao, they talked to me like I'm their errand boy. Hell, I don't work for them. We're not to mess it up. We're not to louse up any evidence. We're not to give out anything to the press. They will take over the inquiry. They are conferring with the Soviets. This is classified."

"Who did you talk to there?"

"The top man. A half hour after we sent them the picture, they telephoned me."

"And?"

Wainwright looked at Masuto and grinned. "I told them that a murder had taken place in Beverly Hills, and as chief of the plainclothes division of the Beverly Hills police force, I was following routine procedure."

"He must have loved that." Masuto permitted himself a slight smile.

"He loved it."

They were at the police station now. Masuto stopped to talk to Joyce. She looked pleased with herself.

"The yellow Cadillac," she told Masuto, "is a Carway rental. It's a two-door 1976 convertible, the only one they have, and they had a fit when I told them it was a police inquiry. I told them not to worry about their car."

"You told them that?"

"Indeed I did. Because just before I called them, the L.A.P.D. phoned in that they had found the car."

"Where?"

"Parked downtown at a meter in front of the public library. Not a scratch on it, but it was ticketed for overtime."

"But you didn't tell them to do a fingerprint search?"

"Sergeant Masuto, it just happens that I did. Now what do you think of that?"

"I think you're wonderful, and you also have blond hair and blue eyes. And I'd guess you're about five feet eight inches?"

"I am, but what has that got to do with anything?"

"That is what I'd like to know," Masuto said.

In his office, the phone was ringing. It was his wife, Kati, and he was suddenly worried. It was rarely that she called him at police headquarters.

"Masao," Kati said unhappily, "they sent Ana home from school with a sore throat."

"Is that all?"

Illness in one of the children terrified Kati. "All?" she cried. "She has a hundred and one degrees of fever."

"Then perhaps you should call the doctor."

"I want to, but it's so expensive. Twenty dollars for a house call."

"Don't worry about the money. Call the doctor."

"Trouble?" Wainwright asked, coming over to Masuto's desk.

"Ana's sick. When I was a kid, a doctor made a house call for three dollars. Now it's twenty."

"A different world, Masao."

"L.A.P.D. found the yellow Cadillac."

"Where?"

"Downtown L.A. They're dusting it."

"Why don't we talk about this, Masao?" Wainwright demanded. "I get nervous as hell when you're holding back."

"I'm not holding back. I just have a package of wild guesses that don't fit. As soon as something fits, I'll let you know. I asked Gellman to have them shake down the hotel until he finds the fat man's clothes."

"He won't. He's so damn nervous already that he's not going to do anything to shake the place. Anyway, we know who he is. What's so important about his clothes?"

"Where they are."

"Well, we don't know that. What about Stillman's wife?"

Masuto picked up the phone and asked Joyce to put him through to police headquarters in Las Vegas. "Who do you know there?" he asked Wainwright.

"I know Brady, the chief. I'll talk to him." He took the phone from Masuto, and a moment later he was asking for Chief Brady. Masuto watched him thoughtfully as he said, "Tom, this is Wainwright in Beverly Hills. One of your citizens, feller by the name of Jack Stillman, was shot to death at the Beverly Glen Hotel this morning." Pause. "No, we got nothing, no motive, no suspects, absolutely nothing. He's married to Binnie Vance, the exotic dancer." Pause. "Yeah, at the Sands, you say. Good. Get someone to break it to her, will you? We'll hold the body until we get her instructions. Thanks."

As he put down the phone, Officer Bailey came in and informed them that a man called Boris Gritchov was outside in the waiting room. He handed Wainwright a card, which stated that Boris Gritchov was consul general in San Francisco of the Union of Soviet Socialist Republics.

"Bring him in here," Wainwright said. "And be damned nice to him, and then keep your mouth shut about his being here."

Gritchov was a tall man, well-dressed, in his early forties, with iron-gray hair and pale gray eyes. He did not offer to shake hands with either of the policemen, and when Wainwright offered him a chair near Masuto's desk, he appeared to accept it reluctantly. His eyes traveled around the room with its bare walls, its pale green paint, and its painted steel furniture. When he spoke, it was with barely a trace of an accent, and he wasted no time with formalities.

"I would like to see a picture of this man who you say drowned."

Masuto opened his desk drawer, took out a picture of the drowned man, and handed it to the Russian. He stared at it thoughtfully, but with no change of expression that Masuto could detect. Masuto gave him points for that. If the Russian had anything to give, it would not come by accident or through an emotional lapse.

"I would like to see the body," he said slowly. "Is it in your morgue?"

"We don't have a morgue," Wainwright said. "We have an arrangement with All Saints Hospital, and we use their pathology room and morgue."

"Isn't that strange for Los Angeles?" the Russian asked. "I always understood that Los Angeles had a large and efficient police force and sufficient violent death to warrant a morgue." He underlined his question with a thinly concealed tone of contempt.

"We are not Los Angeles. This is the City of Beverly Hills."

"But this is Los Angeles," the Russian insisted.

"Los Angeles County, yes," Masuto explained. "The county contains a number of cities, including Los Angeles. It's true that most of Beverly Hills is surrounded by the City of Los Angeles, but we are nevertheless an independent city with its own police force." He felt almost like a character in *Alice in Wonderland*, explaining local geography to a man who has just discovered that a colleague and countryman of his was dead. "May I ask you whether you can identify the man in the photograph?"

"You are Japanese?" Gritchov asked.

"Nisei, which means an American born of Japanese parents."

"And a policeman."

Masuto directed a warning glance at Wainwright, who appeared ready to explode, and then said softly, "So very sorry, Consul General, but America is a place of ethnic diversity which, unlike your country, makes no claims to ethnic purity."

Gritchov's face tightened slightly, but he kept his tone as polite as Masuto's. "You know very little of the Soviet Union."

"Ah, so, I am sure. But I was not thinking of the Soviet Union but of Russia. But I may be mistaken. If so, you have my profound apologies. Nevertheless, would you be kind enough to tell us whether you know the man in the photograph?"

"I would prefer, if you will, to have this whole matter taken under the auspices of the Los Angeles Police Department."

"That's impossible," Wainwright said shortly.

"Then I would like to see the body immediately. I also believe, Captain, that no formal request of the Soviet Union in a matter like this should be dismissed as impossible by a petty bureaucrat."

"If you will wait outside for a moment or two, Mr. Gritchov," Wainwright said slowly, as if each word choked him, "I will have Detective Sergeant Masuto take you to All Saints Hospital."

Gritchov nodded and left the office, closing the door behind him, and Wainwright burst out, "That lousy son of a bitch! Petty bureaucrat!"

"I think we both behaved with admirable control, Captain."

"And we continue to. And for Christ's sake, cut out that Charlie Chan stuff. He's no fool, and I don't want any backwash. Take him over to the hospital. I'm going up to talk with the city manager."

"Right."

"And don't push it. If the goddamn F.B.I. wants it, let them have it." At the door he paused. "You still think that hooker in the hotel killed him?"

Masuto shrugged and nodded.

"Screw the F.B.I! Petty bureaucrat! That bastard!"

4
THE F.B.I. MAN

Riding the mile that separated the police station and All Saints Hospital, the Soviet consul general was rigidly silent, and Masuto made no effort to engage him in conversation. As they entered the pathology room, Dr. Baxter unbent from over the corpse of Jack Stillman, and grinned malevolently at Masuto.

"Back again with a live one," he said.

"Got the bullet?"

"All wrapped up nice and neat. Thirty-caliber short. Pop, pop! Sounds like a stick breaking, so I guess you won't find anyone who heard it. Do you want it?"

"Please," said Masuto.

Baxter handed him a little packet, the bullet wrapped in tissue, which Masuto placed in his jacket pocket. "This is Mr. Gritchov."

Gritchov was observing the action with interest. He showed no signs of being disturbed by the contents of the pathology room.

"Oh?" Baxter raised a brow.

"I would like to take him into the morgue for identification."

"You already know his name. You just told me." Baxter grinned again.

"Very funny. Where's the body?"

Baxter led the way to the morgue door, but as he started to enter, Masuto barred his way. "We'd like to be alone, Doctor—if you don't mind."

"Alone with the dead. How touching!"

"If you don't mind."

"I have no objection, and I'm sure the corpse has none."

Inside the morgue room, Gritchov said, "You're an interesting man, Detective Sergeant Masuto."

"All people are interesting, Consul General, if you regard them without judgment."

"And do you?"

"I try to." He pointed. "There is the body."

Gritchov went to the table and drew back the sheet that covered the fat man. Masuto watched as he stood there, studying the face of the dead man. Then Gritchov replaced the sheet.

"You know him?" Masuto asked.

"Yes. His name is Peter Litovsky. He had a small post in the embassy in Washington. He was what we call a cultural attaché, one who maintains—"

"I understand the function of a cultural attaché."

"Shocking," said Gritchov, with nothing in his manner or

tone to indicate that it actually was shocking. "I shall have to inform his family, and that will not be pleasant."

"Then you know him personally?"

"Of course. I had dinner with him two nights ago."

"Then he was in San Francisco? I thought he was attached to the embassy in Washington."

"He is. Of course. He came to San Francisco with the Zlatov Dancers. That was entirely within his proper function as cultural attaché."

Puzzled, wondering what had changed an angry, taciturn Russian official, who opened his mouth only to deliver thinly veiled insults, into this almost affable conversationalist, Masuto decided to press his advantage and confessed to being somewhat confused by the fact that Mr. Gritchov had refused to comment on the photograph.

"One wishes to make certain in a serious matter like this."

"Naturally. Do you know what Mr. Litovsky was doing in Los Angeles?"

"In Beverly Hills, as you pointed out to me, Detective Sergeant. Beverly Hills is very much spoken of, even in our country. I suppose he seized this opportunity to see how the very rich live in a capitalist country. We have no equivalent of Beverly Hills in our country, so it is quite natural for a visitor from the Soviet Union to be curious about it. What an unhappy thing that he had to pay such a price for his curiosity."

"Do you know whether Mr. Litovsky could swim?"

Gritchov shrugged. "Evidently not."

"Perhaps you do not remember, but when we spoke on the telephone, I told you that Mr. Litovsky was found naked and drowned in the swimming pool."

"Yes. Of course."

"I see. Is it the custom in your country for men to swim naked in a public pool?"

"You mean he had no bathing suit?"

"That's exactly what I mean. Furthermore, his clothes, his eyeglasses, his wristwatch, his wallet—all of these things have disappeared. Furthermore, his drowning was not an accident. He was murdered."

Masuto saw the small muscles around Gritchov's jaw tighten, but his voice was even as he said, "Can't we leave this place, Detective Sergeant? It's cold and the air is fetid."

Masuto led the way out. Baxter had left, and the two bearded young men working in the pathology room gave them only a passing glance. In that place, death was more interesting than life.

"Where can I take you?" Masuto asked when they were in his car.

"I have a reservation at the Beverly Wilshire."

"Then you're staying in Beverly Hills?"

"For the time being."

"Permit me to say that I am somewhat bewildered. I inform you that a colleague of yours was murdered under very unusual circumstances, that he was left to drown naked in a swimming pool, and you have not even the curiosity to ask me how he was murdered."

"How was he murdered, Detective Sergeant Masuto?"

"He was given chloral hydrate, probably in a drink, and then when he went into the pool area, probably because he was choking for air, a person or persons unknown pushed him into the pool and saw to it that he drowned. Then they undressed him and left his naked body floating in the pool, a shameful and ignominious end to any life."

"Detective Sergeant Masuto," Gritchov said quietly, "you are a small and unimportant public official, the equivalent of what we in our country would call a militiaman. You neither function in nor understand a larger scheme of things. I am a diplomat, with diplomatic immunity. I am not called upon to answer any of your questions. There are men in your country who have both the experience with and the responsibility for what happened to Mr. Litovsky last night, and I am sure that they will take the appropriate measures. I think that closes the subject."

For once, Masuto envied Wainwright's choice of language and response. "So sorry, Consul General," he said. "Most humble apologies."

Gritchov said no more. Masuto dropped him at the Beverly Wilshire Hotel in Beverly Hills and then drove back to police headquarters. Sy Beckman was in the office, and he said to Masuto, "Wainwright's in a lather. What got him so pissed off?"

"The Soviet Union. We had a visit from the consul general."

"Oh?"

"He charmed us all. What did you come up with in Stillman's room?"

"Zero. He smokes dollar-fifty H. Upmann cigars. Had half a box there, and I only accepted one of them. It is hell to be an honest cop. Nothing else worth mentioning—not one damn thing. You'd think that if he had a hooker in the room last night, she'd drop a bobby pin or something. Nothing."

"Prints?"

"You know Sweeney. He got enough prints to keep him busy for a week."

"How about Stillman's prints?"

"L.A.P.D. is working on them. Look, Masao, I am starved. Suppose we knock off and go out and eat."

"Order sandwiches and coffee," Masuto said with some irritation.

"What's bugging you?"

"This whole thing. No motive, no reason, no clue, no sanity, and the fat man's clothes."

"Masao, you know Freddie Comstock's a bonehead. Let's you and me shake down that place ourselves."

"Maybe later." He took the tissue-wrapped packet out of his jacket. "Here's the bullet that killed Stillman. Send it down to ballistics and see what they make out of it. I'll order the sandwiches. And then come back with the past ten days of the L.A. *Times*. What kind of a sandwich do you want?"

"Anything that chews."

Masuto ordered the sandwiches, and Beckman returned with a foot-high pile of the Los Angeles *Times*. He had learned from experience not to question Masuto's methods, however far out in left field they happened to be.

"We go through them," Masuto said, dividing the pile in two. "Page by page."

"That will take a month."

"No. Skip the classified and the ads." He thought about it for a moment. "Skip the sports, theater and financial. Stick to the news. Never mind the columns and the editorials, just the news."

"What are we looking for? The Russians again?"

"No, I don't think so."

"Then what?"

"I'm not sure. Something that connects."

"Goddamn it, Masao, I go along with you, but this is crazy. What connects?"

"I don't know, but there has to be something. An important Russian secret agent is murdered. The call comes from Stillman's room. Stillman is murdered. They both knew something, and whatever they knew is going to happen very soon."

"So we look for something that connects. Great."

"Let's say something as meaningless as all the rest of it. Odd. Different. Then we'll try to fit it together."

"You're the boss." He grinned suddenly. "Masao, suppose it happened already? That lets us off the hook."

"That's a thought," Masuto agreed. He picked up the phone and asked Joyce to get him Mike Hennesy in the city room at the Los Angeles *Times*.

"Mike," he said, "this is Masuto over in Beverly Hills."

"Great!" Hennesy exclaimed. "Masao, what in hell goes on up there at the Beverly Glen Hotel? We got a drowning and a murder—"

"Hold on!"

"Masao," came Hennesy's pleading voice, "it's the big story today. Come on—"

Masuto put down the phone, and shook his head. "Start on the papers." The phone rang again. It was Hennesy. "You know I can't peddle information, Mike. Talk to the captain."

"Four fires in a single day in West Covina," Beckman said. "The police suspect arson. Nothing else even shows signs of anything. Here's another one about the agrono-mists. The leader of the group is Ilya Moskvich. Leading agronomist in the Soviet Union. Nobel Prize four years ago."

"Interesting."

Wainwright walked in and stared at the pile of news-papers. "Never mind, I won't ask," he said. "This is what the city pays you for."

Masuto nodded without replying.

"I heard from Vegas," Wainwright said.

"Oh?"

"They can't locate his wife. Stillman's wife."

"I thought she was performing at the Sands."

Beckman looked up and said, "Binnie Vance?"

"That's right. Stillman's wife."

"They got a great police force there in Vegas. Almost as good as ours. They can't locate Binnie Vance, who's only opening tomorrow night here in L.A."

"How do you know that?" Wainwright demanded.

"I'm reading the papers. She opens tomorrow night at the Ventura, that new hotel downtown with the round glass towers." He turned to Masuto. "Does that connect? It's true it's in the theater section, but what the hell, you notice things—"

He paused. Masuto was there and yet not there. He was sitting rigidly, his eyes half closed, and Beckman and Wainwright exchanged glances. Then Masuto said quietly, smiling slightly, "Captain, how do you feel about murders in Beverly Hills?"

"You know damn well how I feel about murders anywhere."

"Yes. The Russian was unpleasant. They apparently have a very centralized system, and they have a low opinion of underpaid policemen like myself. However, if you insist that this is our case, I think that Sy and I can clear it up in the next twenty-four hours."

"You got it."

"And what about Stillman's prints?"

"He was clean as a whistle," Wainwright said, "which don't mean a thing except that he's never been caught."

"And the prints on the yellow Cadillac?"

"They're working on it." At the door, he paused and said forlornly, "The F.B.I. character should be at the airport about now. It's been one beautiful day, and it's not over."

"It's not over," Masuto agreed.

"Did it connect?" Beckman asked.

"What?"

"Binnie Vance."

"Keep looking."

"Two German shepherd attack dogs found dead, poisoned, in the Altra Kennels at Azuza?"

"No."

"Masao, give me a clue."

"I haven't any."

"How about this: 'Jewish Defense League denies theft of four ounces of lead azide, stolen from the Felcher Company in San Fernando.'"

Masuto was suddenly alert. "What date?"

"Four days ago. What's lead azide?"

"Read the rest of it."

"Yeah, here it is. Lead azide, a volatile form of detonator explosive. They reported the theft to the San Fernando police. Whoever took it scratched the letters J.D.L. on the metal container."

"Convenient."

"Well, it made ten lines on page eight. What the hell—four ounces of explosive."

Masuto pushed the papers aside. "Come on, Sy, let's go for a ride."

"Where?"

"San Fernando."

"What makes you think this is a connection? I don't see it."

"Neither do I, but I am sick and tired of sitting here. Anyway, it is time I saw my uncle, Toda."

"Who the hell is your Uncle Toda?"

"My father's younger brother. He has ten acres of oranges outside of San Fernando. Do you know, the land's worth about forty thousand dollars an acre now. That would make my uncle a rich man, but he says that until he dies, the orchard will not be disturbed."

"You grew up around there, didn't you?"

"Before the war. The Valley was like a garden then, no subdivisions, no tract houses, just miles of pecan groves and avocado groves and orange groves. My father used to compare it to Japan. He would say that a place like the San Fernando Valley could feed half the population of Japan. Of course, that was an exaggeration, but that's the way the people from the old country felt about the Valley."

They were on their way out when Masuto caught Wainwright's eye. The captain was talking to a neatly dressed man, gray suit, blue tie, pink cheeks, blue eyes, sandy hair, a man in his forties whose face retained the bland shapelessness of a teenager's. Wainwright motioned to Masuto.

"This is Mr. Clinton, Federal Bureau of Investigation."

Since Clinton did not extend his hand, Masuto made no offer of his. As he examined Masuto, the old gray flannels, the shapeless tweed jacket, the tieless shirt, his cold blue eyes belied the blandness of his face.

"This is Masuto?" he asked Wainwright.

"Detective Sergeant Masuto."

"I hear you grilled Mr. Gritchov?"

"Grilled? No, sir, that's hardly the word. I asked him a few questions."

"Where in hell do you get your nerve? Gritchov is a diplomatic representative of a foreign country, with which at the moment we are in process of most delicate negotiations. He has immunity. How dare you question him."

"So sorry," said Masuto. "It simply happens that another representative of the Soviet Union was murdered in a city which employs me as the chief of its homicide division."

"Peter Litovsky drowned. The kind of loose talk and thoughtless statements you just indulged in could have the most serious consequences."

"Yes, he *was* drowned," Masuto admitted. "He did not drown, he was drowned. There is a specific semantic difference. I would like you to note that, Mr. Clinton. I am not accustomed to loose or thoughtless statements."

"Who the devil do you think you're talking to, Masuto?"

"A federal agent. I'm quite aware of that. But you are in Beverly Hills in the State of California. The fact that Peter Litovsky was a Soviet intelligence agent makes him your problem. The fact that he was murdered in Beverly Hills makes him mine."

"How do you know he was an intelligence agent?" Clinton demanded.

"I told him," Wainwright said.

"Who gave you the right to? The information given to you was classified."

"Masuto's the head of Homicide. Beckman works with him. I felt they ought to know."

"You felt?"

"That's right. I felt. And what are you going to do about it, mister?"

"All right. I know the kind of people I'm dealing with. But let me tell you this, and these instructions come from the top. Litovsky drowned—an accidental death. That's what the newspapers will print, and that's what you will back up. And Mr. Gritchov will stand on the same ground."

"All right," Wainwright agreed. "We cooperate with the federal authorities. Frankly, I don't give a damn what the newspapers print or what you tell them. But I do give a damn when people come into my city and murder, and as far as I am concerned, Litovsky was murdered and I intend to find out who did it."

"We are taking over the investigation. I'll expect your cooperation."

"I'm honored," said Wainwright.

"We can do without the sarcasm. I'll see you later, Captain Wainwright."

He stalked out of the room, and Wainwright muttered, "That shithead. That miserable shithead." When Masuto and Beckman started to follow, he snapped, "Where are you two going?"

"To San Fernando."

"What for? The country air?"

"You don't need us, Captain. You have the whole F.B.I. working for you. In fact, you don't even have a crime. You have an accidental drowning."

"Don't get cute with me, Masao. I've had just about all I can take today."

"I think we're on to something—maybe."

"You don't want to tell me. I might know what's happening in this department if you did."

"I don't know myself. Something about some explosive that was ripped off in San Fernando a few days ago. I don't even know how it connects. I just have a feeling that it does."

"Why don't you call the San Fernando cops and talk to them?"

"I need the fresh air."

"The cutes. Everyone has them today. What about this Binnie Vance? Do you want us to find her and tell her?"

"I'd rather you didn't. I'd rather tell her myself. I'll do that tonight."

"For Christ's sake, Masao, her husband's dead."

"I imagine she knows that by now."

"Where do you think she is, in that new hotel downtown?"

"Probably."

"Well, we got to inform her. It's procedure. You know that."

"Right."

"When can I expect you back?"

"Two hours. No more than that."

As they walked out to Masuto's car, Beckman said to him, "I sure as hell admire your control, Masao. Maybe it's Oriental or something. That second-rate putz!"

"I try not to respond to fools."

"You know, Masao, these shmucks who work for the F.B.I., they get maybe double what we do."

"I suppose I have heard that word a hundred times. Sy, just what is a shmuck?"

"It's Yiddish for a flaccid penis."

"And a putz?"

"Yiddish for an erect penis."

"A remarkable language," Masuto said thoughtfully.

5

THE RELIGIOUS MAN

People who have spent half their lives in Los Angeles are still unable to solve the jigsawlike relationship between the City of Los Angeles, the County of Los Angeles, and the dozens of independent communities that exist both within the city and within the county. Like Beverly Hills, the City of San Fernando is an independent community, but it lies in the San Fernando Valley, entirely surrounded by the City of Los Angeles, an arrangement that succumbs to reason only because it is factual. By freeway, it is some fourteen miles north of Beverly Hills, and all the way there, Masuto remained silent, lost in his own thoughts, grappling with a puzzle that was no more susceptible to reason than the civic arrangements that existed in Los Angeles County. Intermittently, he remembered that he had not called Kati to inquire about Ana's sore throat, and that caused him small twinges of guilt.

They were almost in San Fernando when Beckman, who knew Masuto well enough to respect his silences, asked where they were going, to the Felcher Company or to the cops?

"I imagine the company's closed for the day. We'll talk to the cops."

"Masao, this clown from the F.B.I., he never asked one word about Stillman."

"Perhaps no one told him."

"That's not very patriotic."

"No, I guess it isn't."

"Masao, do you know any of the San Fernando cops?"

"I don't think so."

"There's a fellow called Gonzales who used to be with the Hollywood Division. He switched to a better job with the San Fernando cops. I think he's the chief of detectives or something like that."

They turned off the freeway at San Fernando Road, and a few minutes later they parked at the police station, an old, battered building in the Spanish style. It was almost six o'clock now, but the summer sun was still high, and the shimmering valley heat was only now beginning to break. The cop at the desk told them that Lieutenant Gonzales was down the hall, second door to the right.

They knocked and entered. Gonzales, a heavy-set, dark-skinned man, had his feet up on the desk. He was smoking a cigar and reading a copy of *Playboy*. He grinned at Beckman and shook hands with Masuto.

"Still working for the rich?"

"The pay is regular," Beckman said.

"What brings you up this way? I hear you run a busy little hotel down there, with a drowning and a murder."

"Already?"

"The news gets around. What can I do for you?"

"Four days ago, someone broke into the Felcher Company and stole four ounces of lead azide. We're curious."

"Why?"

"The truth is, I don't really know," Masuto confessed. "We're groping in the dark. We have a situation where nothing connects, and I'm trying to connect it. Maybe it's a gut feeling more than anything else. What about this Felcher Company?"

"They're a small outfit on the edge of town, a chemical company that specializes in detonator explosives."

"Are they clean?"

"As clean as mother's wash. If you're gonna fault them on anything, it's their security system. That stinks. They never had any trouble, so they just coasted along on the proposition that they never would. Not even a night watchman."

"How did it happen?"

"Someone snipped the padlock on the wire fence around the building and forced a window. No alarm system, would you believe that?"

"I'd believe it."

"All that was taken were the four ounces of lead azide."

"Just what is lead azide?" Masuto asked him. "I know it's some kind of explosive, but what exactly? You don't hear about it."

"It's a son of a bitch. The way it was explained to me, a detonator explosive is sensitive. It goes off easily. And this lead azide is nasty. According to the manager, even a contamination by dust could set it off. Just take a stone and let it drop on this lead azide—bang, off it goes."

"And what could four ounces do?"

"Blow us out of this room. They tell me that they use a single grain for a detonator."

"How much is a grain?" Beckman asked.

"Seven thousand in a pound, I think," Masuto said.

"God almighty."

"You know, they keep it in a sort of refrigerator, a temperature control room they call it. That's locked too, and the door was jimmied. And down in the right-hand corner of the door, they scratched the same three letters, J.D.L. The kind of thing you might not even notice if you didn't look. I couldn't make head or tail of it, but one of the men at the plant had been reading about this Jewish Defense League, and so that's how it got into the papers. Me, I just don't believe in crooks that leave calling cards, and anyway we don't have no Jewish Defense League here, and when the cops put out some inquiries in L.A., the people in that outfit were as indignant as hell. Funny thing, this stuff is never used as an explosive. The bomb squad in L.A., they don't come up with anything either."

"Any leads?"

"Absolutely nothing. Felcher's a small outfit with only fourteen people working there, and they all come out clean."

"Yet it had to be someone local."

"We got only one thing in that direction, and it leads absolutely nowhere. They got nice landscaping in front of the plant and they use a Chicano gardener, name of Garcia. He's an old guy, and lived here for years and clean, plain, quiet life, never been busted for anything. Every now and then he picks up a kid to help him, mostly Chicano kids.

Two weeks ago, this guy asked for a few days' work. Said he was broke and he'd work for ten dollars a day. He works out a day and then never shows again."

"Any name?"

"He says his name is Frank. No last name, and Garcia didn't push. About twenty years old, five seven or so, dark hair, dark skin, dark eyes, maybe a hundred and thirty pounds, and that's it. No leads, no trace, nobody else seems to remember him. Yeah, he had an accent."

"Spanish?"

"No. Not Oriental either. Garcia's sure he wasn't Spanish. Garcia heard him muttering to himself, and it wasn't Spanish. You want to talk to Garcia?"

"No," Masuto said after a moment. "I think you got everything there was to get. Anyway, I have an uncle who grows oranges near here, and I want to see him before it gets dark."

"Toda Masuto? Is he your uncle?"

"You know him?"

"The real estate guys would like to put out a contract on him. He has some of the best land around. Say hello for me."

The road to Toda Masuto's neat white cottage was lined with orange and lemon trees, and when Masuto parked in front of the house, the little old man and his wife came out to greet Masuto and Beckman with a delight that their formality hardly concealed. When the bowing and the exchange of courtesies and the family inquiries were completed, Toda said, "Well, sonny, what brings you here?" He had been born in Japan, but he had only the faintest trace of an accent. Masuto had told Beckman that

Toda was past seventy, but he was skinny and vigorous and worked in his groves every day. They sat at a small lawn table in front of the house. Mrs. Masuto had gone into the house and now emerged with a tray containing a teapot, cups and cakes. Toda poured the tea, his eyes twinkling as he looked at the two men.

"Two detectives. Either you've come to arrest me, or the real estate trust hired you to beguile me off my land. May I say, with sincere apologies, such is not possible. So very sorry. The land remains in groves until we die. Then my unworthy son, who teaches physics at Stanford, may do with it as he pleases. However, I shall leave the house and two acres of land to your mother, who has always been my favorite sister-in-law."

"That's very generous of you, Uncle," Masuto replied. "But I come merely to talk about oranges."

"So?" Now he smiled. "You will stay a week perhaps?"

"All my apologies. A half hour at the most. Is the subject so complicated?"

"More than you might imagine. The history of the orange alone could consume hours of pleasant instruction."

"I recognize the value of such instruction, and I have no desire to be disrespectful, and at another time I shall be honored to listen. For the moment, I seek only to know why the Soviet Union should send five agronomists to Southern California and to Florida to seek instruction in the art of growing oranges. Incidentally, the leader of the group is a Nobel Prize winner, by the name of Ilya Moskvich."

"The answer is simple."

"Oh?"

"The Russians do not know how to grow oranges."

"They have sent spaceships to the moon."

"Ah, so. Truly. They still do not know how to grow oranges."

"I find that difficult to believe," Masuto said respectfully.

"Naturally. You consider the growing of oranges to be a simple matter. You go into the supermarket, you select your fruit, and you buy it. Simple, no? No. In fact, there are only four places in the world where they understand oranges. Actually three. I include Spain, because they are very good at the Seville orange, which goes by the technical name of *aurentium*. That is the sour orange, which the English are so fond of for their marmalade. But we must also credit the Spanish for rootstock, excellent rootstock, and that is important. Because you see, nephew, all of the finest oranges are budded. This is a process which you might think of as grafting. We select the most excellent strains and bud them onto proper rootstock. But actually the art of growing fine table oranges is confined to three countries— Japan, the United States, and Israel. In Japan they favor the mandarin orange, which they can for export. That, of course, is a generic name. There are many varieties. In Israel, they grow a fine large fruit, which is a variation of sorts on our navel orange, the unique table orange which is distinguished by the small fruit within the fruit. In Israel, as in America, they specialize in the sweet orange, Valencia, navel, pineapple, Washington, Hamlin, juice oranges in Florida, table oranges here in Southern California—those are our favorite varieties, excluding of course the native mandarins—"

Masuto and Beckman exchanged glances hopelessly, and now Masuto seized his opportunity, "Of course, Uncle."

"Ah, so. A new note of respect?"

"Yes. Oh, yes," Masuto admitted.

"If I were to hold forth on rootstock alone, we could be here until midnight—for instance, the miracle whereby the rootstock of the sour orange increases the sugar content of the sweet orange that is budded upon it."

"I am certain."

"Or the means by which the Japanese raise oranges in a climate hardly suited to them."

"I look forward to that, but not today. I am interested in the Russians."

"Ah, so, I forget that you are a policeman. Well, what I said to you is a fact. I have spoken to growers who have been to the Soviet Union, invited there, as a matter of fact. The Russians are desperately eager to grow good oranges in the Crimea. They used to import oranges from Israel, but now they are very angry at each other. Why the Russians do not have a talent for this, I don't know. I have met few Russians. I know that it is difficult to say anything kind about the Russians, but in one way they are superior to us."

"And what is that way, Uncle?"

"They treasure their agronomists. They are among their most honored citizens. So if they sent five agronomists here, headed by this Nobel Prize man, then they are very serious about oranges."

Mrs. Masuto, who had sat quietly, replenishing teacups throughout the recitation, now smiled with pleasure and informed them that they must stay for dinner.

"I am so sorry," Masuto said. "I am devastated. Accept my most humble apologies. But it would be impossible. We must return to Beverly Hills."

In the car, driving south, Beckman complained about Masuto's refusal of the dinner offer. "I'm starved, Masao, and anyway I'm crazy about Japanese food."

"It might have been roast ham, and if we had not stayed for an hour after the meal, it would have been a breach of courtesy."

"Well, the old man certainly knows his oranges. Why were we there, Masao?"

"Just a notion."

"Goddamn, I'd like to have an acre of that land waiting for me when I retire. It's pure gold. Well, your mother gets two acres, but you're out in the cold."

"Oh, not at all. There are two acres for me in his will."

"Then why didn't he mention it?"

"It would have been most discourteous and thoughtless. It would have placed me in the position of a greedy nephew who desired his death. No, he couldn't possibly mention it."

"That's one way to look at it," Beckman admitted.

Masuto drove on in silence for a while, and then he asked, apropos of nothing, "Are you a religious man, Sy?"

"What?"

"I mean, since you're Jewish, you might belong to a synagogue."

"That's another matter entirely. You got kids, they got to have a bar mitzvah. It's a matter of teaching. Religious? Well, we go on the High Holy Days. I ought to go more often, but you know the way it is."

"Then you belong to a synagogue?"

"I belong. Why?"

"I'd like to talk to a rabbi. How about the rabbi at your place? Would he talk to me?"

"He'll talk to anyone. You ever see a rabbi who didn't like to talk?"

"Where's the synagogue?"

"On La Cienega, south of Wilshire."

"Would he be there now, or at home?"

"Let's see—today's Thursday, and if I remember that's the sisterhood night. They meet at eight, so he should be back at the synagogue by seven-thirty. It's just seven now. What do you want to talk to him about?"

"Jews."

"Why don't you talk to me?"

"I thought I'd get an expert opinion."

"I figured maybe you wanted to be converted. You know, its a thing in Japan now. I was reading how a whole group of Japanese went and settled in Israel. You know, they tell the story about the Jewish tourist. Wherever he went, he'd look up the local synagogue. So he comes to Tokyo and he looks up the local synagogue and goes to the Friday night service. When the service is over, he goes up to the rabbi, tells him he's a Jew from New York. The rabbi looks at him and says, 'That's funny. You don't look Jewish.' "

He waited. "You're not laughing," he said to Masuto.

"I appreciate it."

"Maybe you didn't get the point. You see, the rabbi was Japanese, and when he looks at this guy—"

"I got the point."

"But you're not laughing."

"I told you, Sy, I appreciate it."

"Maybe it's a question of a Jewish sense of humor—" Beckman began, and Masuto burst out laughing. "Now what's funny about that?"

It was just a few minutes after seven-thirty when they reached the synagogue. "You know, my wife's going to be here," Beckman said, "and the kids are at home raising hell by themselves, and she hasn't seen me since three o'clock in the morning when the captain woke me up, and she's going to burn my ass, so let's get out of here before eight by a side door or something, and anyway I am half asleep, and God almighty if I get woken up tonight, I quit this lousy job."

They were told that the rabbi was in his study. They walked through the foyer of the synagogue and down a hallway, and Beckman opened the door for Masuto. It was a pleasant room, walls lined with books, a desk, and behind the desk a round-faced man with glasses. He rose as they entered. "Seymour," he said to Beckman, "this is a nice surprise."

"Seymour?" Masuto whispered.

"This is Detective Sergeant Masuto," Beckman said hastily. "Rabbi Schineberg."

"Sit down," the rabbi said, indicating two chairs on either side of his desk. "Masuto. Nisei, yes?"

Masuto nodded.

"Beverly Hills police. Interesting. We're becoming civilized. What can I do for you gentlemen?"

"He wants an expert opinion about Jews," Beckman said sourly.

"Then you shouldn't come to me. I'm totally biased. I like Jews. That's how I earn my living."

"The fact is," Masuto said, "that I want to talk to you about the Jewish Defense League."

"I understand them but I don't approve of them," the rabbi said unhappily. "They're the result of history, and in my opinion, they're most often misguided."

"You can take the rabbi's word for that," Beckman said.

"You know members of the organization personally?"

"Some of them."

"What do they stand for, Rabbi? What is their purpose?"

"You know that they believe in militant action—for the most part in favor of easing Soviet emigration standards for the Jews who wish to leave. They hold on to the memory of the holocaust of World War Two, the slaughter of six million Jews, as their central focus, and they believe that only by their militant and sometimes, unfortunately, irresponsible protests can they be effective."

"How militant?"

"Well, I'm sure you've read reports in the newspapers."

"Tell me this—do you believe that members of this organization could take part in a cold-blooded, premeditated murder?"

"No! Absolutely not!"

"Why not?"

"It's unthinkable. I know so many of them. They're hotheaded, excitable, but premeditated murder—no."

"What about you, Sy?" he asked Beckman.

"You wanted an expert opinion."

"I got it. Give me your nonexpert opinion."

"I agree with the rabbi."

"Rabbi," said Masuto, "do you have a colleague in Las Vegas who is a personal friend of yours?"

"That's an odd question. It happens that I do. Rabbi Bealson at the Conservative Temple in Las Vegas is an old friend."

"Well, I have a request as odd as the question, and I would not make it except that I am very tired and trying to prevent something from happening that could be very terrible, and without knowing what I am trying to prevent or what will happen."

The rabbi thought about it for a long moment, and then asked, "How do you know it will be very terrible?"

"Because I have been a policeman for many years, and because I learned to sense things. That's not a very good answer, is it?"

"Tell me something, Sergeant Masuto, are you a Christian or a Buddhist, or perhaps simply a person without any particular faith, as so many are these days?"

"I am a Zen Buddhist."

"Interesting. What is your request?"

"I would like you to call your friend in Las Vegas and ask him whether he knows a man, a booking agent, named Jack Stillman."

"Why should he know him?"

"Stillman lives in Las Vegas. I think he's Jewish."

"Still, Las Vegas is a large place. It seems a most peculiar request."

"If you feel it's out of line—" Masuto spread his hands.

Both Beckman and the rabbi stared at Masuto for a few moments. Then the rabbi consulted his desk directory, found the number he wanted, and dialed it.

"Rabbi Bealson, please," he said. And a moment later, "Larry, this is Hy Schineberg in Los Angeles." Pause. "Yes, too long. But you'll have to make it here. My congregation watches me too carefully for me to get away to Vegas." Pause. "No, I'm calling at the request of an interesting policeman. Do you happen to know a Jack Stillman? He lives in Vegas and he's a booking agent." Now the rabbi listened. "Now that is odd, very odd indeed. Thank you, Larry." Pause. "Soon, I trust."

He put down the telephone and stared at Masuto, smiling slightly. "Well, Sergeant Masuto, the world is full of interesting coincidences."

"I don't think that what you are going to tell me is a coincidence."

"Do you know what I am going to tell you?"

"I can guess. I would probably be wrong."

"All right, let's see. First of all, Jack Stillman is Jewish. He is not a member of Rabbi Bealson's congregation, although he was, very briefly, when he married his first wife, whom he recently divorced. Shall I continue, or would you like to guess?"

"Would one of you please tell me what this is all about?" Beckman demanded.

Masuto liked the rabbi. A part of Masuto's life was a game, and he had the feeling that the rabbi understood this particular game.

"Let me guess. Stillman was connected with the Jewish Defense League."

"A theatrical booking agent? Wouldn't that be a strange connection?"

"Perhaps."

"You're an interesting man, yes indeed. The fact is that about a year ago, some J.D.L. youngsters came to Stillman, and he gave them five hundred dollars. It was not a secret. I mean, it was nothing that Stillman attempted to hide, so I violate no confidence. Rabbi Bealson happened to hear about it. He also told me that recently Stillman married an exotic dancer—I think that's the term—whose name is Binnie Vance. She was one of his clients, and she was apparently well known in certain circles."

Beckman was staring at Masuto, his mouth open.

"Is something wrong, Seymour?" the rabbi asked.

"I'll be damned," Beckman said slowly.

"Did he say anything in particular about this Binnie Vance?" Masuto asked.

"No, except that she is an exotic dancer. He did say that Stillman was the last man you would expect to support the J.D.L., but you can never tell about Jews. Could I ask you why you are so interested in Jack Stillman, Sergeant, or is it none of my business?"

Beckman looked at Masuto, who nodded slightly. "He was shot to death this morning," Beckman said. "In his room at the Beverly Glen Hotel."

"Oh, I didn't know. I'm so sorry. What an awful thing—and how terrible for his new wife."

"I should have told you before," Masuto said. "I didn't mean to make light of it."

6

THE
EXOTIC
WOMAN

It was a quarter after eight when they reached the station house in Beverly Hills. Beckman checked in and then went home to sleep. Wainwright had left for the night. Masuto telephoned his wife.

"How's Ana?" he asked.

"She's fine. Her throat seems to be better. Should I send her to school tomorrow, Masao?"

"I don't see why not."

"I'm glad you said that. There's only a few days of school left before the summer vacation, and she loves to go to school. Will you be coming home now?"

"Not now, I'm afraid. Later."

"How much later? Masao, you hardly slept. Have you had dinner?"

"Yes," he lied.

"I watched the television news about that awful thing

that happened at the Beverly Glen Hotel. Please be careful."

"I'm always careful. You know that, Kati."

Frank Cooper was in charge of the plainclothes night shift, and Masuto asked him whether Wainwright had found Binnie Vance.

"She's staying at the Ventura. She opens there tomorrow."

"I know that. Did he reach her?"

"She's opening the Arabian Room, first show on the opening night, and this got to happen. You know what I hear, I hear there's big Arab money in the Ventura, but that could be a crock. You don't hear of nothing these days except that there's big Arab money in it. I don't care how much loot these Saudis got, they can't own everything."

"What I want to know," Masuto said patiently, "is whether she was informed of her husband's death."

"Yeah, according to the captain."

"What was her reaction?"

"Damned if I know. I didn't talk to her."

"What about the Stillman case? Anything new?"

"Nope. But that F.B.I. guy, Clinton, he was here about an hour ago and sore as hell because he couldn't reach you. According to him, you should have been sitting here waiting for him. They're cute, those cookies. He wants you at the Feds' office downtown at eleven tomorrow. He was pissed off because you never mentioned Stillman to him. He wanted to know what kind of idiots we were not to think of a connection between the drowned man and Stillman, especially when the call came from Stillman's room in the hotel."

"What did you tell him?"

"I told him I was a stranger here myself, and that I don't get to work until six o'clock. Anyway, he wants you to bring everything you got on the case with you tomorrow. I guess he don't have a high opinion of the Beverly Hills police."

Masuto left the station house and drove downtown. He took Santa Monica Boulevard to Melrose Avenue, and from there he turned south on the Hollywood Freeway. The Ventura Hotel was clearly visible as he approached the downtown area, and Masuto reflected that it was indeed an incredible building. It consisted of four round towers, like four turrets of some ancient castle, with the body of the hotel seemingly suspended in the center; but the towers were of glass, shining in the night, with outside elevators crawling up and down the glass surface like black beetles. Improbable anyplace, the building was even more improbable here in this earthquake country, and Masuto wondered, as he had so often in the past, at the insistence of engineers and architects that the new Los Angeles be built mostly of glass. The hotel was part of a complex of new skyscrapers that had risen out of the clearance of some of the worst slums in the city, sitting on a hill that had once been climbed by a cable car known as Angel's Flight.

The hotel, still minus the finishing touches of construction, was open to the public, the Arabian Room being the first of its large dining and entertainment rooms to open. The lobby of the new hotel was crowded. It was the end of June, and already the tourist flow into Los Angeles had begun.

Masuto went to the desk and asked for the number of Binnie Vance's room.

"She's not there," the desk clerk said. "Miss Vance is rehearsing in the Arabian Room."

"Where is the Arabian Room?"

The clerk looked at Masuto, a tall, long-limbed, tired Japanese man, hatless, tieless—and shook his head firmly.

"No, sir. It's not open to the public."

Masuto showed his badge.

"That's Beverly Hills—"

"You want the Los Angeles cops?" Masuto snapped. "I'll have them here in the lobby in five minutes, if that's what you want. I want to talk to Miss Vance about her husband. Now use your head."

"About her husband. Yes, sir. Terrible thing. You go up the escalator at the left. You'll see the sign."

"Thank you."

He had almost lost his temper. The day was too long, and he was tiring, and it was no good for a policeman to tire. It was only eighteen hours since Wainwright had awakened him, but it seemed to Masuto that days had been compressed into that time. He had not tasted food since the lunchtime sandwich in his office, and he desperately desired a hot bath, steaming hot, and after that thirty or forty minutes of quiet meditation where he could look into himself and turn away from a world that was at best half mad. Well, very soon now.

There was the Arabian Room, and Masuto wondered why in this day and age in America a hotel would establish a nightclub so named, unless, indeed, there was Arab money invested in the hotel. Certainly it would not surprise him, but then, he reflected, very little surprised him these days.

He pushed open one of the double doors and entered. The room was shaped like a slice of pie, three tiers of tables sloping downward, with the stage where the point of the slice would be. The dominant colors in the decor were red, black, and silver, with tassels, crescent moon, and paired scimitars as a motif. In a pit between the tables and the stage, a four-piece orchestra played. Three men sat at one of the tables, and on the stage a woman in a body stocking undulated to the rhythm of the music. She moved slowly and sensuously, every movement controlled, calculated, exaggerated for the utmost sensual effect.

One of the three men at the table saw Masuto, rose, and walked back to the entrance where the detective stood watching.

"We're closed, mister," he said to Masuto. "We don't open until tomorrow. And tomorrow we're sold out." He was a large, fat man with an unlit cigar clamped in his teeth.

"Who are you?"

"I'm the manager. Who are you?"

Masuto took out his badge. "Detective Sergeant Masuto. I have to talk to Miss Vance about what happened at the Beverly Glen Hotel this morning."

The man's tone changed. "Look, Officer, Miss Vance knows all about what happened in Beverly Hills this morning. It knocked the crap out of her, but she took it. Don't make her take any more of it. Not tonight."

"The show must go on and all that?"

"You're damn right, and thank God she's a trouper. We put out twenty thousand dollars' worth of advertising on this opening—TV spots, radio spots, and the press. We're sold out for three shows, and believe me, they ain't coming to see no Arabian Room. They're coming to see Binnie do her belly dance."

As if taking the cue, one of the two men at the table down front stood up and called out, "Okay, Binnie, that does it for the opening. We'll take a few bars of the belly dance and then we'll wrap it up."

She had come down to the edge of the stage, and both Masuto and the manager turned to watch her. She was not a tall woman, but she had a full, voluptuous figure—without being fat or even plump. She had brown hair that fell to her shoulders. Masuto thought her eyes might be green; at this distance, he was not certain.

"Stillman didn't hurt it none. Just more publicity. It adds up, like a snowball rolling downhill."

"I'm sure Stillman is grateful for that."

"What is it, Officer? You got a bone to pick? The kid's trying to turn a buck. She pays her own way. So lay off her."

"What's your name, manager?" Masuto asked coldly.

"Peterson."

Binnie Vance was doing the belly dance now. Watching her, Masuto said, "Well, Mr. Peterson, I'm here to talk to Mrs. Stillman. I intend to. So when she's finished, you will go over and tell her that."

"Who the hell do you think you are, mister? In the first place, you're a Beverly Hills cop—"

"Just knock that off, Mr. Peterson. If you knew the law, you would know that I can go anywhere in this county in the investigation of a crime. Now I am provoked and I am tired, so if you interefere with me in any way, I'll pull you in for impeding the investigation of a crime."

"You wouldn't—"

"I would."

The music finished. Binnie Vance came down from the stage, and Masuto saw her talking to the two men who had remained at the table. Peterson walked down the aisle and joined them. He pointed to Masuto. They talked softly, too softly for Masuto to hear what they were saying, and then one of the two men who had remained at the table raised his voice.

"Bullshit! You don't have to say one goddamn word to him!"

Binnie Vance tossed her head, the hair flowing around her shoulders; she picked up a light coat from a chair, and walked up the aisle toward Masuto. The three men watched her but didn't move.

"You're the Beverly Hills cop?" she said to Masuto, a faint, almost undefinable accent in her voice.

"That's right, Mrs. Stillman. Detective Sergeant Masuto. I'm the chief of homicide in Beverly Hills."

"Call me Miss Vance. I was Miss Vance a few weeks ago. Now I'm Miss Vance again. I didn't have time to get used to the other one." There was a bitter edge in her voice. It was not a sweet voice. It rasped, and Masuto decided that she had been wise to choose dancing.

"Very well. Miss Vance."

"How about a drink? I need one."

"That would be fine."

"Can a cop drink on duty?"

"I'll go off duty when we start drinking. I've had a long day." She noticed small things, Masuto decided. She was an alert woman. He also realized that her eyes were green, an unusually vivid green.

"There's a bar on the main floor," she said, and when

they were on the escalator, she said to him, "Help me on with my coat. You don't walk around here in a body stocking."

He held the coat for her.

"What do you think of this place?"

"Interesting."

"L.A. is the pits for me, but this place gets to me. I like it. It's wild."

Masuto nodded.

"You don't agree?"

"Well, as I said, it's interesting."

"That's a pissy word. They want to knock an act, they say it's interesting. Here's the bar. You want a table?"

"If you don't mind," Masuto said.

He led her to a table in a corner. It was not a very active bar at this hour. "What will you have?" he asked her.

"A cognac."

He motioned to a waiter, and ordered two cognacs. She was studying him curiously, a slight smile on her lips. Her lips were rather thin, and she wore no makeup, no lip rouge. The dark skin was sunburned, the underside of her chin much lighter. She was pretty, he admitted to himself, and then revised the thought. Handsome was a better word. Her face was square rather than round, with sloping, flat cheeks and a square chin.

"What are you?" she asked. "Chinese? Japanese? Korean? I hear L.A. is lousy with Koreans."

"Nisei," he replied.

"Nisei?"

"That means my parents were born in Japan."

"Then you're a Jap," she said, making the remark deliberately and provocatively.

"If you wish to think of me that way," Masuto agreed, unperturbed. The waiter returned and set down the two brandies. Masuto raised his glass.

"To you, Mr. Japanese detective," she said.

"And since we are being ethnic, what are you, Miss Vance?"

"What do you mean, what am I?"

"You weren't born in this country."

"How do you know that?"

"By your accent."

"I don't have an accent."

"Ah, but you do," Masuto said gently. "Ever so slight."

"All right. I was born in Germany. I left at the age of fourteen, but I thought my English was near perfect."

"It is," Masuto agreed approvingly.

"Why don't you stop being such a hotshot superior Oriental and say what you're thinking?"

"And what am I thinking?"

"That I must be a completely heartless bitch to be sitting here and talking like this and not shedding one damn tear a few hours after my husband was killed."

"No."

"No what?"

"That's not what I was thinking. I was thinking what an extraordinarily beautiful set of movements you went through up there on the stage. You're a remarkable dancer."

She paused, swallowed the retort that was on her lips, and stared at him. "Thanks."

"I meant it."

"Okay, but let's get one thing straight. I wasn't in love with Jack Stillman. All right, I didn't hate him, but I didn't love him. Now he's dead and I'm alive. What should I do? Wrap myself in mourning? I don't have to lie to anyone."

"Not even to me," Masuto agreed. "Why did you marry him?"

"Can I have another brandy?"

Masuto motioned to the waiter. She sat in silence, playing with her half-empty glass until the waiter put down the second brandy. Then she finished the first, dipped her finger in the second one and licked it off.

"You wouldn't understand," she said.

"Try me."

"You know what I got for dancing last week at the Sands?"

"I can't imagine."

"Fifteen grand. For five performances. Fifteen thousand dollars. Before I met Jack Stillman in Vegas, I did club dates and lousy stag affairs for peanuts."

"And he was responsible—for your success?"

"He booked me, and he gave me an image. I can't deny that."

"Then you owed him a good deal?"

"So he owed me. It works both ways. He took fifteen percent off the top and expenses."

"And that's why you married him, because he was responsible for your success?"

"I was responsible for my success, Buster, make damn sure of that. Anyway, I don't have to explain to you why I married Jack Stillman. I had my reasons. I married him."

"No, you don't have to explain. By the way, Miss Vance, when did you leave Las Vegas?"

"This morning. On the eight o'clock plane."

"One day of rehearsal here? Is that enough? I don't know much about such things."

"With that combo in there, it's enough. They're good."

"Do you have your ticket?"

"What do you mean, my ticket?"

"Your airplane ticket."

"No, I threw it away."

"You know, Miss Vance, we can check the passenger list."

"I'm afraid not. I came in on Vegas West. It's a shuttle service. Anyway, what the hell is this? You said when you drink that you're off duty. When you come right down to it, I don't have to answer any questions."

"I only thought it might be easier if you did, here. It's a convenient place for you. It would be tiring to go up to Beverly Hills. By the way, did you know that your husband was staying at the Beverly Glen Hotel?"

"Of course I did. He always stays there."

"But I should think that with you opening here, he would stay at the Ventura. As you are."

"He hated downtown L.A. Anyway, I like to be alone when I'm dancing."

"Do you have any notion who might have shot him?"

"No. None."

"Did he have enemies?"

"A man like Jack, well, what do you think? But not to kill him." She stood up suddenly. "Excuse me for a moment." And she walked off, pausing only to exchange a few words with the waiter.

The moment her back was turned, Masuto took out his handkerchief, folded it carefully around the brandy glass, and slipped the glass into his jacket pocket. The waiter came to the table and said, "The lady won't be back. She's tired. And by the way, we don't give away our glasses."

"It's a memento," Masuto said. He gave the waiter ten dollars. "Keep the change."

"Keep the memento," the waiter said.

Masuto walked into the lobby of the hotel, dropped into a chair, and looked at his watch. It was almost ten o'clock. A long, long day. He turned it over in his mind, trying to remember the events of the day and put them into proper sequence. It was Beckman who caught the piece in the paper about the Russian agronomists. No one else had mentioned them. Was it a three-day visit or a four-day visit that they were making to Southern California? According to Toda Masuto, three days were hardly enough to scratch the surface of the art of orange growing. The Russians could build spaceships, but they couldn't grow oranges. Americans could grow oranges better than anyone in the world, but they couldn't keep their cities from disintegrating. It occurred to him that he had told Beckman to find the agronomists, but then the thing happened to Jack Stillman and they were all there, Beckman and the others, and both he and Beckman forgot about the agronomists. It was a crowded, disorganized day, and that was his fault. He had gone off on a wild goose chase to San Fernando, because someone had stolen some lead azide. Why? What sense did it make? The whole country, no, the whole world was bomb crazy. It had been in his mind all the time. Why hadn't he simply told Beckman to look in the papers for the makings of a bomb? Was it true, he asked himself, that he liked to be mysterious, or was there an undercurrent in his thoughts that he himself was hardly aware of?

He looked up, and there, standing in front of him, was Binnie Vance. She had changed into a yellow pants suit.

"Hello, cop," she said to him.

"I thought you were tired."

"You were the tired one." She dropped into a chair next to him. "I was kind of pissy with you, wasn't I?"

Masuto shrugged.

"I gave you the impression that I didn't give one damn about Jack. That isn't true."

"Oh?"

"You know anything about Vegas?"

"A little."

"Jack lived in Vegas fourteen years. He was an operator, and he spent a lot of time in the casinos. That's why he never had a nickel. When you got a crush on the crap tables, you got an expensive habit."

"I suppose so."

"You don't spend all those years like that and not get mixed up with the Mob."

"And was Stillman mixed up with the Mob?" Masuto asked indifferently.

"He was."

"And you think the Mob put out a contract on him and had him shot?"

"It's happened."

"If that's the case, that's pretty much the end of it."

"What do you mean?"

"Those kind of killings—well, for the most part, they're never solved."

"You mean you don't care about solving them."

"No, we care." He stood up. "Why? Had he run up a score at the tables? Was he a big loser?"

She shrugged. "That's the last thing he'd talk to me about."

"But you'd know. He was your husband."

"I don't know."

"Did you ever hear of the Jewish Defense League?"

"What?"

"The J.D.L., they're called."

"Should I?"

"Your husband was Jewish. You knew that."

She stared at him without speaking.

"You're not Jewish, are you?"

"If it's any of your damn business, no!"

"Well, good night," Masuto said.

7

THE QUIET WOMAN

"In one day," Kati said, "you are everywhere. You see the whole world."

"Not really the whole world, dear Kati." Masuto was steaming in the hot bath he had looked forward to all day, and Kati sat by the tub with two thick white towels in her lap. She was glad that her husband, who was so very American in so many ways, was at least old-fashioned enough to make a sort of ritual out of his bath.

"Only San Fernando and downtown Los Angeles."

"Only San Fernando. That's well enough for you to say. Do you know how long it is since I have been to San Fernando? What can your Uncle Toda think of me?"

"That you are an excellent wife and a devoted mother. What else should he think?"

"That I am an uncaring niece."

"What nonsense!"

"Anyway, I can't understand what took you there. What has Uncle Toda to do with these terrible things that happened at the Beverly Glen Hotel?"

"I had to know why the Russians would send five agronomists to Southern California to study orange growing."

"I could have told you that."

"You could have?"

"Of course. They don't know how to grow oranges. That's all."

"Kati," Masuto said, "you are a remarkable woman."

"I see nothing remarkable about that. It's only common sense."

"When you're a policeman long enough, you tend to forget about common sense."

"Yes."

"What do you mean by that?"

"You never took me to the Ventura Hotel. It's a place that tourists come to see from all over the country, but you never took me there. You're very fine about such things when you're out doing your work, but as far as I am concerned all you desire is an old-fashioned Japanese wife."

"You're not Japanese. You're American."

He stood up, and she opened the towel for him, admiring his strong, long-limbed body. "That's well enough for you to say, but you don't want an American wife."

"That's true. I want you."

"And of course you are too tired to do anything but say that." She covered her mouth, to show a proper exhibition of embarrassment. Then she giggled.

"Too tired!"

"What was she like?"

"What was who like?"

"Turn around, and I will dry your back. That woman you took to the Ventura Hotel."

"For heaven's sake, I didn't take her there. She was there. She's living there. She's performing there."

"Ah, so?"

"You never hear anything I tell you. You just don't listen."

"That's because you only tell me what you want me to know. Did you go to her room?"

"No. What on earth would I do that for?"

"She's a dancer," Kati said smugly. "You see, I do listen to you."

"She's not a woman I would want to have anything to do with."

"Ah, so. And what kind of women do you desire to have something to do with?"

"Kati, this is not like you."

"You see, I have changed. And you still haven't answered me. I asked you what she was like."

"She's well masked."

"You mean when she dances?"

"No, I mean in the Zen sense."

"You know I don't understand the Zen sense, whatever that means."

"I would not like to have this woman as my enemy."

"Perhaps you already do," Kati said lightly. "I think, Masao, that you know women less well than you imagine. You think all women are good."

"Only compared to men. Anyway, I do not like to judge, and good is really a meaningless word. Tell me about Ana. Is her throat better?"

"It's still scratchy. I think I'll keep her home tomorrow. She can play in the sunshine in the garden, and one more day out of school won't hurt. It's better than medicine. Can you imagine paying a doctor twenty dollars for a house call?"

Masuto considered telling Kati that he had just spent ten dollars for three brandies, and then he thought better of it.

"I'll meditate a little now—only for ten or fifteen minutes."

"Oh—will you? Then I am sure I'll be asleep."

"Then I'll meditate in the morning," he replied, smiling. "You see who is the master here."

"I see that you spent the evening with an exotic dancer, whatever that may be—something nasty, I'm sure." She began to giggle, covering her mouth with both hands.

Masuto was awake at six o'clock, refreshed and rested. He put on his saffron robe, leaving Kati still asleep, and went into the living room to meditate. He had often thought of how pleasant it would be to have a small room, walls painted ivory, with no furniture other than a grass mat and a single black meditation pillow, but for a police sergeant with two small children that was impossible. He had a fleeting thought of the two acres that his Uncle Toda would certainly leave him, but he cast that aside. It was an unworthy thought, and in any case, Uncle Toda would probably live for ninety-five useful years.

The meditation took hold. He was alive without moving, listening without hearing, focused entirely on the even rise and fall of his breath. Somewhere, Kati's alarm clock sounded, and then there was the laughter and the muted sounds of the children. As the meditation ended, the room had begun to fill with the delicious smell of crisp, fried bacon.

He ate an enormous breakfast, three eggs, bacon, and two of the fish cakes which Kati had saved from the night before, washed down with two cups of coffee. With Ana protesting against being kept out of school and with the boy dashing through the door to meet the school bus and with Kati glowing in a lovely pink and green kimono, it appeared to be the most normal of days in the most normal of worlds, and Masuto reflected that although his work now and then took him into the depths of a nightmare, he was nevertheless the most fortunate of men.

With that kind of glowing thought, he could not resist the temptation to spend at least fifteen minutes in his rose garden. There he found chafers, which must be removed, one by one by hand. Chafers—and he was already late. Groaning, he abandoned the roses and went out to his car. It took him awhile to get his mind off the subject of chafers and onto the curious jigsaw puzzle of the previous day.

Beckman was already in the office when Masuto arrived, his feet on his desk, drinking coffee from a container and eating a piece of Danish pastry.

"Sy, you remember yesterday I told you to catch up with the agronomists?"

"Yeah, but then Stillman got himself scragged, and we never caught up with anything. Anyway, it says here in the *Times* that they're pulling out on the five o'clock flight for Miami."

"And what about the clothes?"

"What clothes? You want some of this Danish?" Beckman asked him.

"No, it's poison. The Russian's clothes. The drowned man."

"Yeah, that. I called Fred Comstock this morning as soon as I got in. He hasn't turned anything up."

"He wouldn't."

"Right. He's a living proof that the body can survive after the brain dies. What difference do the clothes make now, Masao? We know who he is."

"I don't give a damn about the clothes. It's where they were hidden and why they were hidden."

"They'll turn up."

"Perhaps. Sy, get Sweeney in here, will you, and tell him to bring whatever he has."

Small, skinny, truculent, Sweeney watched Masuto carefully remove the brandy glass from his handkerchief.

"Going to offer me a drink, Sergeant?"

Masuto grinned at Sweeney. "Why don't you sit down?"

"Why the hell are you being polite to me?"

"I am always polite to you," Masuto said.

"You," said Sweeney, "are why I don't miss a confession, so I can tell the priest that I dream of cutting your throat. You would abolish me. You are the clown who is always telling the press that fingerprints are a crock. Now you want favors."

"I have seen the light," Masuto said humbly.

"That'll be the day."

"Sweeney," Masuto said, "I admire you. You are the most professional part of this department. Even the L.A. cops downtown say that you're better than anyone they have."

"Bullshit."

"Ask Beckman."

"That's right," said Beckman. "That's what they say."

"Well, goddamn it, I know my business."

"I know you do. Now tell me, did you find anything in Stillman's room that matches up with what the L.A. cops took off the yellow Cadillac?"

Sweeney grinned.

"You did?"

"Kind of surprised, aren't you?"

"What did you get?"

"One print. Second finger, I think. But both of them are good, clear prints and they match."

"Good. Good. Maybe the right hand?"

"I think so."

"Great. Now take this glass, and see if you can come up with another print that matches the two you have. It's a possibility."

Sweeney nodded. "You think you're on to something?"

"If I am, I'm going to credit you big, Sweeney. I mean that."

"Just show respect, Masao. That's all I ask."

"You have it. Now listen, Sweeney, do the L.A. cops have a machine that can transmit prints to Interpol?"

"If it's a machine, they got it."

"They can send pictures," Beckman said, "so they can send prints."

"What else did you pick up in the room that isn't Stillman's or the chambermaid's?"

"I got three good ones," Sweeney said.

"Put them through to Interpol, and all of them to Washington. The matching set, the car and the room—put them through to the New York cops and to Chicago. But all of them to Interpol, and all of them to Washington."

"That's going to cost a bundle, Masao, and you know how the L.A. cops are. They want a guarantee that they're going to get paid."

"Get an authorization from Wainwright."

"He's not here," said Beckman. "He went downtown this morning to meet with the Feds. He said to remind you that the G-man wants you to bring all the records on the case down there at eleven o'clock."

"Get the authorization. I'll sign it myself."

When Sweeney had left to get the authorization, Beckman said to Masuto, "What's this all about, Masao?"

"A lot of wild guesses. I could put them together, but what would it mean? I still have nothing."

"Whose hand was around that brandy glass?"

"Binnie Vance's."

"You don't say." He looked at Masuto with new respect. "When did you see her?"

"Last night at the Ventura Hotel. Would you believe it, ten dollars for three brandies?"

"Is she all they say?"

"She is."

"And you think she killed Stillman?"

"If she did, I'd like to know why."

"She only just married him. That's a quick turnoff."

Sweeney came back with the authorization. Masuto signed it and then said to Sweeney, "Would you do me a favor?"

"Now that you seen the light, yes."

"Stop off at the Ventura Hotel on your way downtown.

There's a man called Peterson who runs the Arabian Room, or if you don't find him, there must be a P.R. office for the hotel. Tell them you want a picture of Binnie Vance, and then have the L.A. cops put it through with the finger-prints."

"To all them places?"

"We might as well."

"Wainwright's going to yell like hell."

"If he's going to have murders, it's got to cost," said Beckman.

"Put it through to the cops in Bonn in Germany too. We might as well go the whole hog."

"You're the boss, Masao."

"You got him eating out of your hand," said Beckman, after Sweeney had gone. "Did the L.A. cops really say that about Sweeney?"

"I stretched it."

"Well, they won't tell him. It's nine-thirty, Masao. What do you want me to do while you're down there with the Feds?"

"Find Litovsky's clothes."

"I'll give it a try. You think this Binnie Vance, being an exotic dancer and hotheaded and full of piss and vinegar, comes into Stillman's room and finds him with that big blond hooker and loses all her cool and kills him?"

"Stillman was shaving. That doesn't sound very passionate."

"You think maybe Stillman invented the hooker?"

"Maybe."

"Funny, in a place like the Beverly Glen Hotel, you don't have to invent. You just reach out and take. So no hooker.

Who was in the room and made the call, Binnie Vance?"

"Maybe. She claims she flew in from Las Vegas yesterday morning."

The telephone rang. Beckman picked it up, listened for a moment, and then passed it to Masuto.

"Masao?" It was Kati's voice, high-pitched, uncontrolled.

"Yes, what is it?"

"Ana's gone!"

"Kati, get hold of yourself! What do you mean, Ana's gone?"

"She isn't here. She's gone."

"Where was she?"

"In the garden. She was there playing with her doll, Masao. Then I turned away for a few minutes. I went into the kitchen—" Her voice broke, and she began to sob.

"Kati! Kati, get hold of yourself!"

"I shouldn't have left her alone. I looked out of the kitchen window, and she was gone."

"Did you look for her? She may have wandered off."

"Masao, it was only a minute or two." She was sobbing uncontrollably now.

"Please, Kati, please. You must talk to me. Get hold of yourself."

"Yes. Yes."

"Now just what happened?"

"I tried—I tried to see her from the kitchen window. Then I went out into the garden. I thought she was hiding. I thought she was playing a game. I didn't know—"

"Kati!"

"So I looked everywhere. Then I began to call her. Then I went out on the street. I ran up and down the street. I looked everywhere. But she's gone."

"She didn't go back into the house?"

"How could she, except through the kitchen?"

"All right. Now look, Kati dear, this is not your fault. I'm sure Ana is all right. I want you to stay in the house. Don't go out looking for her again. Just stay in the house, and I'll be there in ten minutes. Don't talk to anyone about this. Just stay there and be calm, do you understand?"

"You'll find her, Masao, please."

"I'll find her."

Then he turned to Beckman. "Come on, Sy."

"What happened?"

"I'll tell you in the car. Let's get moving."

8

THE
EDUCATED
MAN

Driving through the streets of Beverly Hills, his car siren howling, Masuto knew only that his lovely, pleasant world of the morning had shattered, leaving an empty hole of sheer terror. He had always lived with a simple acceptance of the fact that fear was not a problem he had to face. An old Zen story told of the student who came to the Zen master and asked the question: "Why should I study Zen, Rashi?" to which the master replied, "Because then you will not be afraid to die." Masuto was not afraid to die, but the world was full of many other things that were more terrible than death.

"If we pile up and end up in a hospital, Masao," Beckman said quietly, "you won't be helping the kid any." They had just made a two-wheel braking turn into Motor Avenue off Pico Boulevard and were roaring south toward

Culver City. "Anyway, we ought to think, and I can't think at this speed."

Masuto slowed down. "You're right, Sy," he muttered. "You're right."

"You're sure it's connected?"

"I have a gut feeling."

"A kid could wander out of a back yard and drift away and just get disoriented, and then the kid is lost. It's happened before. It happens every day."

"Not a Japanese child. She wouldn't leave the garden. I know Ana. Kati knows her. She just wouldn't leave the garden."

"Then if she was snatched, you face it and try to think it through. I can't do your thinking for you," Beckman told him, almost harshly. "All day yesterday you ran us in circles, with the damn oranges and the lead azide and all the rest of it. What does it add up to?"

Masuto made no reply, and Beckman said more softly, "I got kids, so don't think I'm not feeling this. But you're a cop, Masao. Now why would anyone snatch your kid? It's not money; you don't have any."

"It's a club."

"Best damn club there is. But if they're going to clobber you, they got to tell you why."

"They will," Masuto whispered. "They will."

The quiet, cottage-lined, neat and sun-drenched street where Masuto lived belied the thought of violence. The houses were owned, for the most part, by Nisei and Chicano families. They were plain, hard-working people who had put their life effort into owning a home on a small plot of land and the houses and the flower-lined lawns underlined the care and pride that went into that ownership.

Beckman remained in the car when they reached Masuto's house. "I'll drift around and see if I can turn up anything," Beckman said. "Just the streets around here. You go in to Kati."

Masuto nodded and ran into the house. Beckman drove off. Kati had been watching for them, and after she let her husband in, she burst into tears. Masuto took her in his arms and rocked her gently.

"Easy, easy, Kati. Ana will be all right. I promise you that."

"Who took her, Masao?"

"Stop crying. You must stop crying. We are going to be very calm, both of us."

"I'll try."

"No, you must. Now go into the kitchen and make tea."

"Tea? Now?"

"Yes, now," he said firmly. "I will go with you, but I want you to make the tea. Mr. Beckman will be here in a moment, and we will give him tea and cake. Have you cake in the house?"

"Masao!"

"The tea now, please."

She bowed her head and dried her tears on her apron and went into the kitchen. Masuto followed her. She filled the tea kettle.

"Now tell me again what happened."

"But I told you."

"Again, very carefully."

"She was playing in the garden with her doll, sitting under the acacia tree. I went into the kitchen to do the breakfast dishes. I cleared the table and put the dishes in the sink. Then I looked out of the window—" She choked up.

"Go on, Kati. Think. Exactly as it happened."

"She wasn't there. First I tried to see through the window. Then I ran outside."

"How long was she out of your sight?"

"Maybe three minutes, no more. I had cleared the table before. Then, after you left, I had a cup of tea while Ana had her cereal and hot milk. Oh, Masao—"

The telephone rang.

"Stay here and finish the tea," Masuto said. He went into the living room then and picked up the phone. It was a singsong voice with a curious accent, a man's voice.

"This is Detective Sergeant Masuto?" the voice asked.

"Yes. Speaking."

"Then you will listen to me very carefully, Detective Sergeant Masuto. She has not been harmed. She will not be harmed—so long as you obey our instructions."

"How do I know you have her? How do I know she's all right?"

As he said this, the doorbell rang. Kati ran through the living room to the door. It was Beckman. He took Kati's hand, and the two of them stood there, watching Masuto.

"I will let you talk to her. But quickly."

"Daddy, Daddy," came Ana's voice, "they broke my doll."

"Are you all right?"

"They broke my doll."

"You mustn't cry, baby, you'll be home soon."

Kati began to sob. Beckman put his arm around her and whispered, "She's all right, Kati."

"That's enough," said the voice of the man. "Listen. About the case of the drowned man, you will do nothing. You will leave it alone. Completely alone. You will do nothing. You will make yourself unavailable to the police, and then if you leave it alone, completely alone, your child will be released at seven o'clock this evening. Otherwise, you will never see your child again." Then a click. It was over.

"Who was it?" Beckman asked.

"The kidnapper."

"What did he say?"

"What did Ana say?" Kati cried. "Is she all right? Why didn't you tell him my child is sick?"

"I think she's all right. She sounded all right."

"Was she crying? Did they hurt her?"

"I don't think they hurt her. She said they broke her doll. No, don't cry anymore, Kati. I told you I will take care of this. I want to talk to Sy now. Would you bring us tea in here, please?"

Kati nodded and went into the kitchen. Masuto dropped into a chair and motioned for Beckman to sit down.

"What do they want?" Beckman asked him.

"As he put it, the case of the drowned man. I imagine that includes Stillman. I am to leave it alone and make myself unavailable to the police. I use his words. If I follow their instructions, Ana will be released at seven o'clock. If I don't, I will never see her again."

"You're sure he said you? You, Masao? One person? He didn't say both of you?"

"What are you getting at, Sy?"

"If he had someone watching the house or watching the station, he would have said both of you. You and your partner."

"Yes. Of course. I'm not thinking." Masuto took a deep breath. "I have to think. I have to think clearly. It's not a game anymore."

"Why do you say game? That's not like you, Masao."

"Game. Yes."

Kati came in with a tray, which she put down on the coffee table. "What do they want, Masao?" she asked pleadingly. "Why did they take my child? We don't have money. Children are kidnapped for money."

"They want me to stop what I'm doing."

"But what are you doing?"

"Kati, do you trust me? I love Ana as much as I can love. But you must trust me. Will you, please? And I will bring Ana back to you today. I promise that."

"And will you stop what you are doing? Will you listen to them?"

"I will find Ana."

"How can you find her?"

"I will find her. I promise you. Now I want you to leave us alone. We must talk."

"What shall I do?" she asked woefully.

"I think you should lie down for a little while. You've had a bad shock. Lie down and rest. There's nothing else you can do for Ana."

She nodded and left the room. Beckman looked at Masuto thoughtfully, and said, "There's been a kidnapping, Masao. You know what the procedure is. We notify the Culver City police, and then we bring in the F.B.I."

Masuto didn't answer. He poured two cups of tea, and

Beckman noticed that his hand did not shake.

"Do you want anything in your tea?"

"No."

Masuto lifted the cup to his lips in what was almost a formal gesture and sipped at the tea. Then he put the cup down.

"You heard me, Masao."

"I heard you, Sy. Here is the way it's going to be. We do not notify the Culver City police and we do not call in the F.B.I. This is for me. If you want to help me, I'll be grateful. Otherwise, you can have out of it."

"That's a lousy thing to say."

"I apologize. I'm sorry. We're in this together."

"And you're making that same stupid mistake that the parents of every kidnapped child make. Ana's seven years old. If she saw them, she can identify them. Do you think there's a chance in the world that they'd let her go alive?"

"Not much chance, no."

"Then what?"

"We have to find her."

"How? Where? If you think this Binnie Vance was involved with the drowned man, then she had help. Is that it? Does she know where the kid is?"

"Maybe. Maybe not. We can't even place her at the Beverly Glen Hotel. She only fits with a lot of guesswork—and there's no reason, no motive, no sense in the whole thing."

"We could pick her up and sweat it out of her."

"Pick her up for what?"

"We could try to sweat it out of her."

"She's not the kind of a woman you could sweat anything out of. You know," said Masuto, "there was something damned strange about that voice on the phone."

"What?"

"Adverbs."

"You just lost me."

"Adverbs. They're part of what makes English an impossible language. An uneducated man faults his adverbs. So do foreigners. The man on the phone said, 'you will listen to me very carefully.' Why didn't he say, listen careful? Then he used the word *unavailable*. That's a fancy word. He could have said, get lost. Stay away. Forget it. Drop it. But he said unavailable. Then the adverb again. Leave it completely alone or something like that. But he said completely."

"What does it add up to?"

"It was a young voice, high pitched. I'll tell you what it adds up to. It adds up to a student."

"And there's got to be maybe ten thousand foreign students just in L.A. alone."

"It's a game!" Masuto blurted out. "It's a crazy, sick, monstrous game. The games children play—the bloody, stupid games! Sy, there's only one way to go. We have to find the drowned man's clothes."

"Why? For Christ's sake, why?"

"For the same reason that they were hidden. Because they make a connection, and right now we have no connection. None. I could make guesses. I could put the whole thing together—or at least I think I could—but now they've pulled Ana into their insane game, and I want my child. I want her alive."

"All right, Masao. It's a quarter to eleven. We have eight hours."

"No. We have five hours."

"Why only five?"

"Four, five, six—somewhere in there, believe me."

"All right, five hours. We got the second largest metropolitan district in the United States. Where do we look?"

"In the hotel. Those clothes never left the Beverly Glen Hotel."

"You're sure?"

"I'm not sure of anything, but that's where we look."

"And right now Mr. Arvin Clinton, the pride of the F.B.I., is sitting in his office downtown waiting for you to show up and kiss his ass."

"We'll just let him wait."

Masuto went into the bedroom, where Kati lay huddled on the bed. He sat down beside her and touched her cheek gently.

"Kati."

"Masao, if anything should happen to her—"

"Nothing will happen to her."

"Or to you. Then I would surely die."

"Nothing will happen to me. I will find Ana and bring her home. I promised that. I want you to stay here. I still have a son, and he will look for his mother when he comes back from school. He is not to know anything about this. No one is. Even if Captain Wainwright calls, you must tell him nothing, except that you do not know where I am. And you must say that to whoever calls."

"Then you will do what they ask?"

"I will do what has to be done." He bent over and kissed her. "Lock the doors. Remain in the house. If the man who took Ana calls again, you must tell him that I am carrying out his wishes."

"And Uraga?" she asked. "What can I tell my son? He will see my face."

"Then you must compose your face. Ura is nine years old. He is old enough to behave like a man and accept the fact that his mother is not always smiling and laughing."

"He will ask about Ana."

"I took her to the doctor. Tell him that, and also tell him that he must remain in the house."

"How do I know he's all right?"

"He's all right. If you wish, call the school, but don't let them know that anything is wrong. I'm sure he's all right. I'll call you later. From here on, Kati dear, every minute is precious to me. Let me depend on you."

She sat up and nodded, her face tear-stained. "Yes, I will do as you say."

9

THE DARK MAN

Masuto was himself again as they got into his car. He said to Beckman, "You drive, Sy. I want to put it together."

"The hotel?"

"Yes, the hotel."

"You know, Masao, when I spoke to Freddie Comstock, he said that he cased every empty room in the hotel, and those that were vacated too."

"Yes."

"Does that mean anything?"

"I don't want to think about it that way," Masuto said. "I want to start from the beginning and put it together. I have all the pieces, or at least I think I have. So just let me put it together, and then we'll see where we are—" thinking to himself that now he must put everything else out of his mind, all his terror about his daughter, Kati's misery, what might be happening to Ana right at this moment, all of it out of his mind and only the puzzle, only the game that sick men played all over the world in this time of his life.

"Go ahead, Masao."

"We begin with a man who calls himself cultural attaché but who works for Soviet Intelligence. He uses the Zlatov Dancers as an excuse to go to San Francisco, I don't think the Soviets give two damns about the Zlatov Dancers, but the only other Russian event on the West Coast that we know about is the fact of the agronomists. That the Soviets care about. They used to buy oranges from Israel. Now they have to learn how to grow their own. So we make our first guess: Peter Litovsky is sent to California to keep an eye on the agronomists."

"Maybe," Beckman said.

"Why maybe?"

"Because the fat man is no bodyguard. He's in his fifties, fat and soft. One punch in his gut would put him out of the running."

"That makes sense. All right, the fat man's an intelligence agent. He comes out here because someone wants a meeting to discuss something concerning the agronomists. That's better, of course. The meeting is set up at the Beverly Glen Hotel."

"Who with?"

"The next guess. Binnie Vance."

"Why?"

"It makes some sense. At least we know that whoever killed Stillman was someone he knew and trusted. You don't walk up behind a man who's shaving and put a bullet into the base of his skull while he's looking into a mirror unless he knows you and trusts you. So from there we make the presumption that she was in his room the night before and that she was the woman who phoned in the news about the fat man."

"And the hooker?"

"She never existed. I never believed she did."

"Okay. We got Binnie Vance as a Russian agent of some sort." Beckman shook his head. "It don't figure. It's that Mata Hari crap. She's just a belly dancer."

"She's German. She doesn't have to be an agent. She could have some connection in East Germany that would bring Litovsky out here to see her."

"All right. I go along, Masao. Now we come to the stopper. How did they get into the hotel? How did the fat man get in? No one saw him. No one remembers him. He never registered."

Masuto smiled slightly, the first time since his wife had phoned him that morning. "Kati was talking about common sense last night. Do you remember, yesterday morning, I told you to go down to the basement and check the bolt on the door?"

"I did. It was open. That's how she got out."

"She never got out," Masuto said. "She was in the hotel all the time. If she killed Stillman, she had to be there. If she drove away in the yellow Cadillac, then she had to be in the hotel."

"And the bolt?"

"Sy, it was opened from the inside, not to let anyone out but to let Litovsky and Binnie Vance in."

"You're guessing, Masao."

"Of course I'm guessing. I haven't got one shred of

evidence to put Binnie Vance in the hotel or even in Los Angeles that night. But Sweeney lifted a fingerprint in the room that matches a fingerprint in the yellow car. So I know that someone who was in that room was also in the Cadillac."

"That makes three of them," Beckman said. "Binnie Vance, someone to drive her and Litovsky to the hotel, and one inside the hotel to let them in."

"Three. It would have to be at least three. Sure, a drugged Litovsky could go staggering out to the pool and even a woman could push him in. Then if she were cool enough, conceivably she could get into the pool with him and undress him while his body floated there. It's possible, but it doesn't make much sense."

"Then what happened?"

"I can make a better guess. Whoever opened the service door for the woman and Litovsky had managed to get a housekeeper's key. That wouldn't be too difficult for someone working in the hotel. He opens an empty room and lets Litovsky and the woman in. They have drinks there, and Litovsky passes out."

"A smartass intelligence agent?"

"You never met Binnie Vance," Masuto said. "I don't know what went on in that room. And what makes you think that intelligence agents are so bright? That F.B.I. man is no shining example of brilliance, and maybe the Russian agents are just as stupid as the Feds."

"Just as horny, you can count on that," Beckman agreed.

"All right. Now they got Litovsky, who's out cold. The man and Vance come back in the room. They have a fat man who weighs well over two hundred pounds. Maybe they walk him down the hallway. Maybe they use a laundry bin or something of that sort to get him to the service elevator. It's probably two o'clock in the morning now, and the hallway is empty. They take him down to the dressing room and undress him. They carry him to the pool and dump him in. They know that Litovsky will be identified, but they decide that undressing him will buy them a few hours, and that's important to them. Then they go out through the service door."

"And why don't they take the fat man's clothes with them?"

"Because they're in Beverly Hills. Because if any one of our patrol cars spots two suspicious-looking people in a car at two in the morning, they might well pull them over. And after midnight, a Beverly Hills cop is very careful. At least, that's the way the myth works, and those two probably know it. And if they have the fat man's clothes, his wallet, his watch and his glasses in the car, then they're finished."

"One loose end, Masao, and that knocks the whole thing apart. If they're that smart—"

"It's not smart!" Masuto snorted. "That kind of sick conniving isn't smart."

"Whatever they are, why didn't Binnie Vance bolt the service door behind them?"

"Two reasons. First, they wanted us to think that the killer had left the hotel." Masuto sighed and shook his head. "It's easy, when you look back."

"And the second reason?"

"Because Binnie Vance wasn't there."

"Where was she?"

"In Stillman's room, watching through the window, waiting for the body to be in the pool long enough for

Litovsky to drown. Either she let herself in with the housekeeper's key, or if the door was bolted, she awakened Stillman and he let her in."

"Then he was awake when she made the phone call?"

"That's right. Probably."

"And when we went to his room yesterday morning?"

"She was there, Sy—maybe in the bathroom, maybe in a closet, but sure as God she was there. I don't suppose we'll ever know what happened during the next few hours. Possibly Stillman decided that he had to tell the truth. Maybe she pretended to go along with him. He went into the bathroom to shave, and she shot him."

They were turning off Sunset Boulevard now, entering the long driveway of the Beverly Glen Hotel. It was twelve minutes after eleven o'clock in the morning.

"No evidence and no motive," Masuto said. "But it's all we have."

Sal Monti opened the door. His grin vanished when he saw Masuto's face.

"Just keep it in front where we can get it quickly," Masuto told him. "Don't park it down the hill."

"A Toyota in front? It makes a lousy—"

"You just damn well do as I tell you!" Masuto snapped.

"All right, all right. Don't burn my ass off."

They went into the hotel. Comstock was sitting in the lobby, reading the Los Angeles *Times*. In an attempt to blend with the surroundings, he wore wide-bottom slacks and a golfing sweater. His shirt was open two buttons on the top. It went oddly with his square face and bristly gray hair. When he saw Masuto and Beckman enter, he jumped up to greet them.

"Anything I can do for you boys?"

"You didn't find the clothes?" Masuto asked.

"No, sir, Masao. I turned this place inside out. You know, you're the second party asked me that today. The Fed was here, bright and early this morning."

"Arvin Clinton, the F.B.I. man?"

"Him and a buddy."

"What did they want?"

"They asked me a few questions, same stuff about yesterday, and then they wanted to see the pool. So I took them down to the pool, and they stood there looking at it for about five minutes. Then they wanted to know what part of the pool the fat man was in. So I showed them. Then you know what they tell me, Masao?"

Masuto and Beckman exchanged glances.

"Tell us."

"They tell me the fat man drowned. I know he drowned, I say to them. So they say to me, no, Mr. Comstock. The word's around that he was murdered. That's dangerous talk. That's the kind of talk that makes a lot of trouble. You're a decent patriotic American, and you don't want to get involved in that kind of trouble. So you just remember that this is an accidental drowning. The fat man falls in the pool and he drowns."

"And then?"

"And then they take off. The funny thing is, I been reading the L.A. *Times* and that's the story they been running, that the fat man drowned by accident."

Masuto nodded. "I guess that's the way it is, Fred. Tell me something, do you know of any hotel employee who didn't show up for work yesterday or today?"

"Jesus Christ, Masao, there got to be maybe a hundred people work in the hotel, with the gardeners and the restaurants and the chambermaids. There ain't no day when one of them don't show up."

"Who runs the bellhops?"

"Artie. That's the big black guy over there."

They walked over to the tall black man, who nodded and said, "I know you, Sergeant. What can I do for you?"

"How many men work for you?"

"I got four good boys."

"Any of them call in sick yesterday or today?"

"No, sir. They are all on the job."

"I'll try the Rugby Room," Masuto said to Beckman. "You go downstairs and do the laundry."

The Rugby Room and the open lanai that was the outdoor connecting part of it was sparsely populated by the last of the late breakfasters. It was still too early for lunch. It was a warm, lovely June day, and the doors to the lanai were wide open, revealing the wrought-iron tables and the pink tablecloths. As Masuto stood there, studying the place, he was approached by Fritz, the mâitre d'hôtel.

"Sergeant Masuto, is it breakfast? As our guest, please."

"I had breakfast. How many people work in your room, Fritz?"

"Bartenders, waiters, waitresses, busboys, the kitchen help—all of them?"

"Yes."

"Forty-two, I think. We overlap because we are open sixteen hours a day."

"Fritz, I'm interested in someone who didn't turn up for work yesterday and today."

"That's every day, Sergeant. If not for goldbricking, I could get by with five people less."

"I'm interested in yesterday and today."

"There's Johnny at the bar. He was out yesterday, but he came in today. Ah—let's see. There is a kid we take on for busboy, maybe a week ago. Look, Sergeant, I don't want no trouble about this. It's hard as hell to find busboys—especially busboys who got more brains than a cow. So we don't ask too many questions when we get one we can use."

"Fritz, I'm not going to make any trouble for you. But this is life and death."

"As serious as that? Sure. Anyway, this kid, he got too many smarts for a busboy. He's not in yesterday. Today, he's on the late shift, starts at noon. Hey, Max," he called to one of the waiters, "is Frank in yet, that new busboy?"

"No sign of him yet."

"His name is Frank—Frank what?"

Fritz shook his head. "I can get it for you."

"Wait. What does he look like?"

"Very dark, black hair. Maybe twenty, twenty-one. Skinny."

"Chicano?"

"No, not Chicano. Some of the boys try to talk to him in Spanish, but he doesn't know Spanish. Some kind of accent, not German or French, because I can spot that. I figure he's some kind of student maybe."

"Fritz," Masuto said, trying to control his eagerness, "the people who work here, they have to come off the street and change into their work clothes. Where?"

"We got a dressing room behind the kitchen."

"Take me there."

"Sure, sure. You think there's something funny about that kid?" He led the way through the cocktail lounge into the kitchen and through it. "You know what kind of trouble we got already? You need a busboy, everyone says there are five million unemployed, but go try to find a busboy. So we can't pick and choose."

"I know, I know," Masuto said.

They were in a narrow room now, a room about twelve feet long, a wooden bench running down the middle and rows of metal lockers on either side. Most of the lockers had padlocks on them. A waiter sat on the bench, lacing his shoes.

"Which is his locker, Fritz?"

"We look. The names are on them."

The waiter stopped dressing to watch them. Fritz was farsighted, fumbling for his glasses as Masuto traced through the names.

"Here!" Masuto cried. "Frank Franco!"

The locker was padlocked.

"I want this opened, Fritz. Now!"

Fritz nodded.

"Now, damn you! Now!"

"Sure, sure." He turned to the waiter. "Steve, go get the handyman."

"What did the kid do? You can't just—"

"Get the handyman," Masuto said, his voice like ice. "I'm a policeman. You have him here in five minutes, or I swear I'll take you in."

"Sure. Okay. I'll get him." He got up, stared at Masuto a moment, then left.

"Fritz, does anyone know anything about this kid? Do you have an address for him?"

Fritz shook his head hopelessly. "All right, you don't hire people this way. He said he was looking for a place to live.

He had just come into town. So I let it go, and a couple of days ago, I ask him again. He says he thinks he got a place—"

"Goddamn it, are you telling me you hire like that? Where was he sleeping?"

"Sergeant, I swear, I'm telling the truth. It happens."

"All right, it happens," Masuto said more softly. "Who did he talk to? Did he make any friends?"

Fritz creased his brows. He was a large, soft man, and he knew he was in trouble. The whole thing frightened him. He had never been at ease with the complex of laws that surrounded hiring, Social Security, withheld taxes, and compensation, and in this particular case he had short-circuited everything. He took out his handkerchief, wiped his brow, and said, "I try to help, yes? I do my best. A few times, I see him talking to Maria."

"Who's Maria?"

"Maria Constanza—she's a good girl, a Chicano. I don't want no trouble for her. She's a waitress. She works in the lanai. In the lanai we have waitresses. She works three years here."

"Is she here?"

"Yes."

"Get her in here."

"All right, I bring her."

As he left, the handyman entered carrying his tool box—a middle-aged man whose blue eyes peered inquiringly at Masuto from behind gold-rimmed spectacles.

"Are you the cop?" he wanted to know.

"Sergeant Masuto, Beverly Hills police. Open this locker for me."

"You sure you got the right?"

"I'm damn sure. Now open it."

He took out his hammer and gave the padlock a couple of sharp blows. It was a combination lock. Nothing happened. "Sometimes you can spring them, sometimes you can't." Then he took out a hacksaw and went to work. He was sawing away at the lock when Fritz returned with Maria Constanza.

She was a slender, pretty girl, with wide brown eyes and a look of fear on her face.

"Maria Constanza?" Masuto asked.

She nodded.

"Sit down please," he said, indicating the bench. "Don't be afraid."

She sat down tentatively, staring at him.

"Would it be better if we talked in Spanish? Would it be easier for you?"

"Por favor," she whispered.

Then he spoke in Spanish. "Don't be afraid. Nothing will happen to you. But if you can help me, a little girl's life might be saved."

"I will try to help you."

"That locker," he said, pointing to where the handyman was sawing away, "belonged to a man called Frank Franco. Fritz tells me that you were friendly with him."

She nodded again. "Yes."

"How friendly?"

"What did he do?" she whispered.

"I don't know—yet."

While they were speaking, Beckman came into the room. He exchanged glances with Masuto, shook his head, and then noticed the handyman sawing away. He stood silently.

"We talked to each other," Maria said. "We had one date. He took me to the movies. We saw the picture called *King Kong*."

"Did he ever tell you anything about himself?"

"A little. He was lonely. He lived with his brother."

"His name was not Frank Franco."

"You know that?"

"What was his real name?" Masuto asked gently.

"Issa."

"Issa what?"

"I don't know." She shook her head. "He never told me. But he said I might call him Issa, not in the restaurant, but when we were alone. He made me promise that I would never reveal his name. Now I've broken my promise."

"You're an illegal immigrant?"

Her eyes filled with tears.

"Don't be afraid, please. The fact that you're an illegal immigrant is no business of mine. Nothing will happen to you. I promise you."

"Please. I must work. I have a little boy who will starve if I don't work. My husband is in Mexico. This is the first man—I can't lose my job, please."

"You will not lose your job." He turned to Fritz. "She's done nothing, Fritz. I don't what her to lose her job."

"She's a good girl. Maria," Fritz said to her, "tell him whatever he wants to know. You won't lose your job."

"This man, Issa," Masuto said in Spanish, "is he an Arab?"

"I don't know. When I asked him where he was from, he just shrugged and said it was far away. He and his brother were students at the University of Nevada. Then they came here."

"Do you know where he lives?"

She nodded. "We stopped by his house that night. He wanted to put on a clean shirt. I sat in the car."

"Where? What address?"

"I don't know." She shook her head. "I didn't see the address. It was on Fountain Avenue, a few blocks east of Western."

"Would you recognize the house?"

"I think so."

"What kind of car did he drive?"

"The locker's open," the handyman said.

"Can I go?" Maria asked tremulously.

"No. Please. Stay here."

"I must go back to the room," Fritz said.

"Yes. Fritz, find someone to take over for her. I want her with us for a few hours."

Beckman was at the locker. "What did she say, Masao? My Spanish is lousy. You asked her if she knew where he lives."

"She thinks she could recognize the house." He opened the locker. There, neatly folded, were a suit of blue worsted, shoes, socks, underwear, shirt and tie, and on top of them a wallet, a notebook, a wristwatch, and a pair of silver-rimmed spectacles.

"You can go now," Masuto said to the handyman. "And just keep your mouth shut about this."

"I got to tell Mr. Gellman that I opened the locker."

"All right. Tell him to talk to Sergeant Masuto about it. And you tell no one else."

He left, and they were alone in the room with the girl, who sat forlornly on the bench.

"Put it all together, Sy," he said to Beckman. "We'll take it with us. Handle the glasses and the watch with your handkerchief. Sweeney may be able to take some prints from them."

Then he turned to the girl. "I want you to help us, Maria. I want you to come with us—just for a half hour or so, and then you can come back here to work."

"What do you want me to do?"

"I want you to show us the house where Issa lives."

"What will happen to him?"

"Whatever he makes happen."

"Will you hurt him?"

"I hope not."

"Should I change my clothes?"

"No, we have no time for that. Just as you are is fine. Come on, Sy."

Beckman, carrying the bundle of clothes, followed them out of the room.

10

THE ANGRY MAN

Beckman drove, while Masuto sat in the back seat of the car and talked to Maria. As they swung up Sunset Boulevard toward West Hollywood, he said to Beckman, "Easy, Sy. I don't want to attract any attention, and I don't want any sheriff's cars or L.A. police pulling us over to find out what we're up to. Just stay on it nice and easy."

The girl was crying again. "I gave you my promise, Maria," Masuto said to her. "I told you no harm would come to you and that I am not an immigration agent." He repeated it in Spanish. "So no more crying. We have only a little time, and you must answer my questions."

"I will try."

He gave her his handkerchief. "Dry your tears. You are not betraying anyone. Do you think that people who murder, who will kill a small child—do you think such people can be betrayed?"

"I don't know."

"Then believe me. Now tell me, before, when you spoke of the car, was that the car he drove you in, this man, Frank?"

"Yes."

"Where was it parked when you left the hotel that night?"

"Down the hill from the service entrance."

"What kind of a car was it? A fine car?"

"A splendid car. A Mercedes. I asked him how a busboy could drive such a car."

"Yes? What did he say?"

"It was not his car. A friend's."

"Did you ask him what friend?"

"He said a dear friend. It made me think it was a woman," Maria said. "I don't know why. I just thought so. And I asked him. He became very angry."

"Did he tell you?"

"No."

"What color was the car?"

"Dark red."

"Did you notice the license plates?"

She nodded. "Yes, the state of Nevada."

"You said he lived with his brother?"

"He said that."

"You didn't see the brother?"

"No. Only Frank—Issa."

They had turned south on La Cienega now, and then left into Fountain Avenue. Beckman said over his shoulder, "I caught that about the red Mercedes. We could find out if Binnie Vance owns a red Mercedes."

"It will all be over by that time, one way or another."

"I could put it on the horn."

"No!" Masuto snapped. "I don't want anything on the radio. I don't want any questions or answers."

"Okay, Masao. It's your shtick."

"Did he say anything about seeing you again—or when?" Masuto asked the girl.

"I did," she replied plaintively. "He was nice."

"Did he say he would see you again?"

"He said maybe. He said he didn't know if he would stay with the job or not. He didn't like being a busboy."

"Him and the brother makes three," Beckman said.

"Yes." Then Masuto asked the girl, "Did he speak of any other friends? Any other brothers?"

"No. No, I don't think so."

"It don't mean they were actually brothers," Beckman said.

"I know. It doesn't matter."

They drove on in silence for a while, and then Beckman said, "We'll be coming up on Western in a few minutes. Maria should start looking. What do you want me to do, Masao?"

"Just easy. About twenty-five miles an hour. When she spots the house, don't stop or slow down."

They passed Western. "It's on this side," said the girl, pointing.

"Don't point. Just watch. On the right, Sy."

"There," said Maria. "That place with the car in the driveway."

"Red Mercedes with Nevada plates," Beckman said.

Masuto leaned in front of her as they passed the house, a rundown frame cottage on a street of rundown frame cottages.

"Turn left up to Sunset on the next corner," Masuto said to Beckman; and then he said to the girl, "We're going to drop you off on Sunset Boulevard, and you can get a bus there back to the hotel." He pressed a five-dollar bill into her palm. "This is for bus fare and your trouble. You helped a little girl to live, and you helped other people too, and I thank you. But I don't want you to say anything about this to anyone. Do you understand?"

She didn't want to take the money, but he insisted, and when they had dropped her off and turned back toward Fountain, Beckman said, "I don't know, Masao, the way you let her go. She could have been tied into it."

"That kid?"

"It happens."

"Not with a kid like that. No. She gave me what she had."

They had turned back into Fountain. "How close?" Beckman asked.

"Find a place to park about a block away. Don't pass it again. I don't want to press our luck."

When he had parked the car, Beckman twisted around to face Masuto. "You know, Masao, we're in L.A. now."

"We have the legal right to go anywhere in the county in pursuit."

"We're not in pursuit."

"I say we are."

"Okay. You say we are. I say we should call the Los Angeles cops."

"Sure. We call in the Los Angeles cops, and they bring the swat team and we have fifty guns around that house with its paper walls and tear gas and the rest of it, and inside you have two half-insane, desperate men who have already been a part of two killings and they're planning maybe a hundred or two hundred more before the day is out, and they're holding my kid as a hostage. Suppose it was your kid they had in there, Sy? Would you call in the swat team? Think about it."

Beckman thought about it for a moment or two, and then he said, "What do you mean, two hundred killings?"

"Just answer my question."

Beckman drew a deep breath and sighed. "All right, Masao. Your way. What is your way?"

"First thing, Sy, take off your gun." He removed his own pistol from the holster under his armpit, and handed it to Beckman. "Lock them both up with the fat man's clothes in the trunk."

Beckman just stared at him, holding the gun that Masuto had given him. "You're out of your mind."

"No, Sy, I'm very sane. That wretched little house is made of matchwood. A bullet would go through the door or even both walls. They could be armed with forty-fives, and a forty-five is like a cannon in that place. If we come in there armed, they're going to start shooting. I can face getting shot; so can you. I don't want my daughter to face it."

"And what in hell do you think is going to happen when we go in there unarmed? Either they kill us or they take us. Then where are we? And how in hell do we get in there? You say the door's made of matchwood—right? We kick it in and get them before they get us."

"And suppose one of them's with Ana?"

"Goddamn it, Masao, we can't go in there unarmed. How?"

"We knock at the door. They open it. They let us in." He was peeling off his jacket as he spoke.

"What's that for?"

"No jacket. No guns. I want them to see."

"They open the door. Then what?"

"We take their guns away."

"What?"

"Now listen to me, Sy. There's no time. Just listen and don't argue. I had a dozen years with the martial arts. I was trained by one of the best in Los Angeles. I can take the gun from the man who's holding it on me. Don't question that. It's you I'm worried about, and I need you because there's two of them. But if you're afraid to try it, I'll try it alone."

"You're damn right I'm afraid. Shit. What the hell. You got any pointers?"

"Yes. These are terrorists. Amateurs. They kill with their demented ideology. They plan and they think in their own demented way. But they're not trained, and when they kill they have to think first. That takes two seconds, one second—even half a second is enough. Hit at the wrist, like this." He made a chopping motion, his palm held flat. "Don't try to grab the gun—just hit at the wrist, and when you make that chop, make it with every ounce of strength in your body. If you hit right, you'll break his wrist. But don't go for the gun. If the gun remains in his hand, kick him in the testicles with all your strength. Watch his eyes. Wait for the moment when his eyes flicker toward me."

"What will you be doing?"

"Don't watch me. There'll be two of them, probably each

with a handgun. If your man has a rifle or a shotgun—that's an outside chance—the same thing, the wrist. I'm hoping that when we're in, they'll tell us to turn around. If they do, you hesitate. I'll turn immediately and use my foot. But don't watch me. Watch the eyes of the man who has a gun on you. Do you think you can do it?"

"No, but what the hell." Beckman peeled off his coat.

"We go in with our hands up. Don't put down your hands. With your hands up, you have a fraction of a second more."

They put their jackets, their guns, and the fat man's clothes in the luggage compartment. The street was empty, as are most streets in Los Angeles in midday. Then they walked down the block to the shabby little house with the red Mercedes in the driveway. Two wooden steps led up to a tiny porch. Both men in their shirtsleeves mounted the steps.

Masuto knocked. No response. He knocked again. Wood creaked. Masuto felt the hot summer sun. He was sweating. Then, a voice.

"Who is it?"

Masuto recognized the voice. It was the voice he had heard on the telephone.

"Masuto. My partner's with me. We're unarmed. I'm playing it your way. We'll stay with my daughter. We're out of it."

"If this is a trick, Masuto, if you have a swat squad outside, the kid will die. First. I swear it."

"No tricks. Just the two of us, unarmed. Alone."

Words in another language. Words replying. He was right. There were two of them—hopefully no others.

"I'm going to open the door, Masuto. You come in with

your hands up. Then your partner, with his hands up. Believe it, mister. Any tricks, your daughter dies."

"I believe you," Masuto said.

The door opened, and Masuto entered, followed by Beckman, both with their hands raised. The man who had opened the door was on Masuto's left. He kicked the door shut and stepped back. He was a slender, dark-faced, dark-haired young man, and he was covering Masuto with a heavy automatic pistol. The room itself was empty, except for some boxes and pillows on the floor. The other man, shorter, heavier, was on the right, pointing a revolver at Beckman. He was about three feet from Beckman as they entered.

"Keep your hands up and turn around, both of you," the thin man said. Masuto turned immediately. Beckman hesitated, watching the eyes of the man facing him, and then the eyes flickered. Beckman never saw Masuto's motion; he was fixed on the eyes of the man covering him. As Masuto turned his back to the thin man, his body unleashed like a spring, and he drove his shoe into the thin man's testicles with a force that threw him across the room. It was more than a karate kick; it was an explosion of all his pent-up, controlled fear and anger and frustration, so violent that he slammed off his feet onto the floor. Beckman, in the same instant, forgot all that Masuto had spelled out for him and hit the man on the right with all his strength. Beckman had been a professional boxer before he became a policeman. He hit the shorter man squarely in the center of his face, feeling the nasal bones crunch under the blow. The man staggered and then collapsed like a sack. Masuto rolled over and grasped the automatic, which had fallen out of the thin man's hand.

The thin man lay huddled across the room, his knees drawn up, whimpering with pain. The other man lay motionless on the floor, blood pouring from his nose. Beckman was clutching his right hand with his left hand.

"God almighty, I broke my hand!"

Masuto handed him the automatic pistol. Beckman took it in his left hand. There were two doors on the right side of the room they had entered. The first opened into a filthy kitchen, with two chairs and a table of dirty dishes and sandwich bags and soda pop bottles. Masuto threw open the other door. It was a bedroom. Two mattresses on the floor, some blankets and a single chair. Ana lay on one of the mattresses, her hands and feet tied, her mouth gagged with a handkerchief. Masuto took off the handkerchief, and Ana began to scream hysterically. Masuto went to work on the cords that tied her hands and her feet.

Beckman rushed into the room.

"It's all right, Sy. Stay with those two bastards."

The cords were off. Masuto took the child in his arms. He was on his knees, rocking her back and forth, clutching her tightly. "It's all right, baby, it's all right now. Everything's all right now. We're going home."

Bit by bit, her screams turned into whimpers. She buried her face in Masuto's shirt, and holding her tightly, he rose and went into the next room. The thin man still lay curled up, clutching his groin and moaning in pain. The other man was unconscious on the floor, his face in a growing pool of blood. Beckman had both the automatic pistol and the revolver stuck into his belt, and he was massaging his right hand and grimacing with pain.

"Sure as God, I broke my hand, Masao. How is she?"

Still holding the child with her face in his shirt, Masuto

took his handcuffs from his back pocket and threw them to Beckman. "Cuff them both," he said shortly, "and stay with them. I'll be back with the car in an hour. She's all right. I'm taking her home.

"This one needs an ambulance," pointing to the unconscious man. "I broke his nose."

"He'll live."

When he put Ana down on the seat next to him in his car, thinking how much she looked like one of those Japanese dolls they sold in Little Tokyo in downtown Los Angeles, with her jet black hair, her straight bangs and her round face, she had stopped sobbing and was able to smile at him and say, "You look funny, daddy."

"Why?"

"Your face is so dirty."

"We'll go home, and we'll both wash, and everything that happened is only a bad dream."

"It was real," she whispered.

"Yes, it was real," he said to himself. "Only too real."

He drove onto the freeway. There was no traffic to speak of at this time of the day, and in exactly twenty minutes he was in front of his house in Culver City. Kati must have been at the window, because Ana was hardly out of the car when Kati had her in her arms.

11

THE EXOTIC WOMAN AGAIN

It was half past two in the afternoon when Masuto returned to the cottage on Fountain Avenue. The two dark men still lay on the floor, their wrists handcuffed behind them, the shorter man with a smashed face that was a bloody mask, blood all over his clothes. Beckman was leaning against the wall with the two guns stuck in his belt.

As Masuto entered, the skinny man started to shout at him in a language that Masuto guessed was Arabic, and then switched to English. "My brother needs a doctor. He is dying."

Ignoring him, Masuto asked Beckman about his hand.

"I don't know, Masao. It hurts like hell. I never hit anyone that hard before."

"Are you animals? My brother is dying!"

In response to this, the man with the broken nose moaned with pain.

"This place stinks," Beckman said. "Can we get them out of here?"

Masuto did not reply. He stood there silent, staring at Issa.

"How did Kati take it?"

Masuto ignored him, staring at Issa.

"If they both died here," Masuto said thoughtfully, "no one would know the difference."

"Masao!" Beckman was shocked. Masuto met his eyes, and Beckman sighed and shrugged. "If you want it that way."

"You wouldn't dare!" Issa screamed.

"What's your name?" Masuto demanded. "Your real name?"

The thin man pressed his lips together.

"Give me the revolver," Masuto said to Beckman.

"It's just a cheap Saturday night special," Beckman observed, handing it to him.

"It works." Masuto spun the cylinder. "It's a rotten gun but it works. I guess that's what one asks of a gun." He pointed the gun at Issa, who cringed and closed his eyes.

"Open your eyes and look at me when I speak to you," Masuto said quietly. "I asked you your name. I am not asking for evidence or anything that may be used against you. I simply asked your name."

"Issa Mahoud."

"And his name?" pointing to the other.

"Sahlah Beeden."

"Then you are not brothers?"

"We are brothers in the struggle for justice."

"And what struggle is that?" Masuto asked.

"The struggle to liberate my homeland from the Zionist pigs."

Masuto turned to Beckman and said, "Read them their rights, Sy."

"This is an admonition of rights," Beckman said tonelessly. "You have the right to remain silent. If you give up the right to remain silent, anything you say can and will be used against you in a court of law. You have the right to speak with an attorney and to have the attorney present during questioning—"

"Stand up, both of you," Masuto said when Beckman had finished.

Issa struggled to his feet. "My brother can't stand up. He needs an ambulance."

"Get him on his feet, Sy."

Beckman dragged Sahlah to his feet, and they marched the two of them outside to Masuto's car. "They'll make a mess of the seat," Beckman said. "Maybe we ought to call an ambulance."

"The hell with the seat," Masuto said coldly. "We deliver these two ourselves."

With Beckman's help, the two men got into the back seat of the car. A few people came out of houses along the street to stand by their doors and watch in silence. The traffic moving by slowed. Masuto opened the luggage compartment, and they put the two guns in there and took back their jackets and their own guns.

At the station in Beverly Hills, Beckman marched the two men inside, Masuto following with the pile of the Russian's clothes and possessions and the two guns. Sergeant Connoley was at the desk. He said, "By God, Masao, we been looking for you and Beckman all day. Where the hell have you been? And what have you got there?"

"Where's Wainwright?"

"He went back to the Beverly Glen Hotel with the G-man. He's screaming bloody murder about the way you and Beckman took off and never called in or one word about where you are. What do you want me to do with these two beauties?"

"Book them and then lock them up."

"For what?"

"Start with this. Murder, accessory to murder, conspiracy to murder, kidnapping, armed robbery, and resisting arrest."

"That's all?"

"Armed robbery?" Beckman whispered.

"We'll get to that."

"Better give it to me again," Connoley said. "It's a long list."

Masuto repeated the charges, and then told Connoley, "We'll be with Sweeney if the captain calls in."

"That one," Connoley said, "ought to go to a hospital. He don't have much face left."

"He can walk," Masuto said coldly. "Get Sam Baxter over to patch him up. I want him here."

"Baxter will love that."

"I don't give a damn what Baxter would love."

Climbing the stairs to Sweeney's office, Beckman said to Masuto, "I never seen you like this before, Masao. It's no good. It's not your way."

"I'm all right."

"You're involved, which is no good for a cop. Ana's with her mother. It's over."

"Not yet. It's not over yet."

Sweeney looked up from his light table as they entered his office and grinned. "Ah, the two missing hawkeyes. It's only three-fifteen. Do you still work here or are you on pension?"

"We have ten minutes, and this is damned real and close, Sweeney. So tell me what you've got."

"Goodies. So many goodies I don't know where to begin. Start with the glass. You consort with belly dancers, Masao, a side of you I never suspected."

"Will you get on with it!"

"This belly dancer, she was in Stillman's room and she was also in the yellow Cadillac. They all match."

"How do you know it was the belly dancer? I never told you that."

"But I have my ways. I got her photograph and I spent the taxpayers' hard-earned money. Washington, nothing. Chicago, New York, nothing. But Bonn in Germany—I hit pay dirt. They sent a Telex back that she was wanted by the cops there under the name of Bertha Hellschmidt, that she was suspected of being an agent of the East German intelligence, and they sent me a set of her prints for confirmation. And, sonny, they matched."

"That's good," Masuto said. "That's wonderful, Sweeney. I'm grateful. Did they say what she was wanted for in Bonn?"

"Something to do with the murder of the Israeli athletes at the seventy-two Olympics. They didn't go into details, except to mention that her father was an SS officer back in the Nazi days."

"Good. One more favor, Sweeney—only because we have no time. We booked two men downstairs. One of them, the skinny one, is called Issa. Get his photograph and send it to the San Fernando cops, care of Lieutenant Gonzales. Get him on the phone and tell him I want him to show the picture for identification to a man called Garcia, who is the gardener at the Felcher Company. Remind him about our conversation yesterday."

"That's all? Don't I get to know what this is all about?"

"I'll buy you lunch tomorrow and tell you the whole story. Oh, yes, one more thing."

"I thought so."

"Call Bob Phillips. He's the chief of security at the airport. Tell him to meet me at the departure gate of National in twenty minutes and to have two of his men with him."

"You can't get to the airport in twenty minutes," Beckman said.

"We're going to give it a damn good try. Come on, Sy."

"What shall I tell Wainwright?" Sweeney called after them.

"Tell him the whole story."

"Whatever that may be," Beckman muttered.

In the car, Masuto driving, siren going, and identification lights flashing, Beckman said plaintively, "It makes no sense, no damn sense at all. An East German spy who is Binnie Vance murders a Russian agent. The daughter of an SS officer who is also Binnie Vance marries a Jew and then kills him. And if I read you, this Issa steals the lead azide and lays it on the Jewish Defense League."

"It wasn't programmed that way. They didn't mean to kill Stillman. He was set up for the Russian's death, and when he didn't follow the script, she killed him. He had the J.D.L. connection. It made sense. It was just a question of time. A few hours more, and every piece would have fallen into place."

"All right. I go along with you. Just tell me why they killed the fat man."

"For one thing, it led to Stillman and the Jewish Defense League. Or maybe he read her too well and told her all bets were off. Or maybe he was a double agent. Or maybe she was. Or maybe he balked at the notion that it was worth blowing up an airplane with over two hundred people on board just to kill five agronomists and lay the blame on the Jewish Defense League and the Zionists. Or maybe he got on to the notion and decided that it was senseless. Or maybe he didn't know one damn thing, and for reasons of their own the Russians decided to get rid of him and sent her to do the job. You can take your choice, Sy."

"Do you think we'll ever know?"

"Maybe. Maybe not."

They were on the San Diego Freeway now, screaming south at eighty miles an hour.

"Better all around if we stay alive," Beckman said casually.

"We'll stay alive."

"I should have called the L.A. bomb squad."

"I don't want them there with that damn truck of theirs. I don't want anything to alarm Miss Binnie Vance."

"It still don't make sense, a woman cold enough to marry a man just to set him up like that."

"She's pretty cold, but maybe when she married him she didn't have that in mind. She could have found out about his big contribution to the J.D.L. and decided that he was a proper candidate. Who knows? I would guess that she planned the whole thing, but why not give her the benefit of the doubt? It's the last benefit she'll have."

"I read a book about that Munich massacre of the Israeli athletes by the Palestinians at the seventy-two Olympics. The East Germans could have saved a couple of them," Beckman said. "Their quarters were right across the street. They didn't. They just watched the whole thing, cold as ice."

They were close to the airport now. Masuto turned off the freeway onto Century Boulevard, and a few minutes later they came to a stop in front of the National Airlines gate. Phillips was already there, waiting with two uniformed airport police. He was a slow-moving, ruddy-faced man, whom Masuto had encountered half a dozen times through the years, and he unhurriedly shook hands with both of them.

"Sy Beckman, my partner."

"What have you got, Masuto?" Phillips asked him.

"You know about the Russian agronomists?"

"Right. We got extra security from here right into the plane." He looked at his watch. "They should be here in about half an hour. Six seats first class on the regular flight to Miami."

"Six seats?"

"They got an interpreter who travels with them. We're trying to keep it very low key. We don't expect any trouble." He looked at Masuto keenly. "Are you bringing me trouble?"

"Some. Any minute now, a belly dancer called Binnie Vance will get out of a taxi or some other car. She'll be carrying a suitcase which will contain four ounces of lead azide and maybe another ten pounds of dynamite or some other explosive. It's probably rigged with an altitude detonator or a time device. She has almost certainly bought a ticket on the plane to Miami, but she has no intention of going there. She'll check the bag through on her ticket, and then go back to the Ventura Hotel where she's the opening act tonight."

"You're putting me on."

"No. I'm giving it to you straight. It's a long, twisted story that we have no time to go into. Just take my word for it."

"You're not talking about a hijack. You're spelling out a plan to blow up the plane and kill everyone on board."

"Right."

"But why?"

"How the devil do I know? A new terror tactic, an excuse to start a war, a tactic for a new wave of anti-Semitism."

"Who's behind it?"

"There too. She's East German. The others are Arabs. Maybe the Palestinians, maybe the Germans, maybe the Russians. They got it set up to lay it on the Jewish Defense League."

"What does she look like?"

"Medium, good-looking, green eyes, dark hair, good figure. I suggest you put your two men over at the baggage entrance, just in case. We'll cover the main entrance."

"She'll be carrying the bag?"

"I think so. That lead azide is volatile. Tell your men to handle with care."

He walked off with the two uniformed police. When he returned, he looked at his watch and said, "Four-ten. The

Russians will be arriving in the next ten minutes or so. The plane boards at four thirty-five. Suppose she doesn't show?"

"Then we'll put them on another plane and go through every piece of baggage."

"That won't be easy."

"It's easier than dying, isn't it?"

"All I got is your say-so, Masuto."

"You got mine," Beckman whispered. "Over there."

A taxi had pulled up to the curb, about thirty feet short of where they were standing. A smartly dressed woman in a black pants suit got out and reached into the cab. The cab driver came around the cab to help.

She gave him a bill. "I'll do it. Keep the change."

She reached into the cab again and drew out a medium-sized Gucci suitcase.

"Is that her, Masao?" Beckman asked softly.

"That's our girl. Let her check the suitcase through. Then we'll take it." Masuto turned his back to her. "She knows me," he explained.

"She's giving it to the luggage porter," Beckman said.

Masuto heard her say, "The five o'clock flight to Miami. Will it be leaving on time?"

"Usually does, ma'am. Could I see your ticket?"

She gave him the ticket, and he wrote her baggage check and handed it to her. Then he took the suitcase and put it on his cart.

"Get the suitcase," Masuto said to Phillips. "We'll take care of her."

"Okay."

"And then have one of your men call the bomb squad."

As Masuto turned around, she was entering the airline

terminal. Masuto and Beckman followed her. "Now?" Beckman wanted to know.

Masuto shook his head. "Let's see what she does."

Keeping their distance, they followed and saw her enter the ladies' room. They stood at the ticket counter, waiting; a few minutes later she emerged and walked to the exit and out to the sidewalk. She went to the curb and waved to a cab. Then they closed in.

"You don't need a cab, Miss Vance," Masuto said. "We'll give you transportation."

Two airport policemen, about forty feet away, stood on either side of the Gucci bag. Phillips strolled toward them.

"Detective Masuto," she said. "How odd—" She noticed the bag and broke off. Beckman cuffed her wrists.

"Damn you, what are you doing?"

"I'm sorry. You're dangerous, lady."

Masuto said, "Mrs. Stillman, I am arresting you for the murder of your husband, Jack Stillman, for the murder of Peter Litovsky, for conspiracy to destroy an interstate airliner, and for the transportation of dangerous explosives. Sy, read her her rights."

"You're crazy!" she cried shrilly. "You're all insane. I'm opening at the Ventura tonight."

"Not tonight. Not any night."

"This is an admonition of rights," Beckman was droning. "You have the right to remain silent—"

"Oh, shut up!" she screamed at him.

Beckman droned on.

"She's a tough cookie," Phillips said. "I bet she's something on the stage. I never saw her dance. Now I guess I never will."

"I'm afraid not."

"Where you taking her, Masuto?"

"Back to our place. When the bomb squad finds out what's in the bag, give me a call and tell me."

"Okay. Sure. I got to take off."

"Why?"

"The agronomists. I got to stay with them."

Masuto, Beckman, and Binnie Vance turned to watch Phillips. Two enormous black Cadillac limousines had drawn up at the curb, and from them emerged the agronomists, their interpreter, several county officials, and Boris Gritchov, the consul general.

"Well, we finally caught up with the agronomists," Beckman said.

"Let's get out of here," Masuto told him.

Beckman took Binnie Vance's arm. She turned on him suddenly and screamed, "Let go of me! Keep your hands off me, you lousy Jew bastard!"

Her shrill cry attracted the attention of the arriving delegation, and they turned to watch Beckman, who, ignoring his injured hand, practically lifted Binnie Vance into the car. Gritchov met Masuto's eyes, and Masuto smiled, bowed ever so slightly, and said, "So very sorry, Consul General."

They were in the car, driving north on the San Diego Freeway toward Beverly Hills, with Binnie Vance huddled in the back seat next to Beckman. Beckman leaned forward and whispered to Masuto, "Do I look that Jewish, Masao?"

"Do I look Japanese?" Masuto said.

12

THE QUIET WOMAN AGAIN

It was five-thirty and Masuto sat at his desk, staring at his typewriter. Beckman sat facing him and rubbing his hand.

"I can't write this," Masuto said. "I don't know where to start. There was too much yesterday and too much today."

"Can you move your fingers if your hand is broken?" Beckman asked.

"Suppose you write the report, Sy."

"How can I type with this hand? Do you think I ought to have it X-rayed?"

"The hell with it," Masuto said. "I'll do it tomorrow. I'm going home. I need a bath. You know, we don't eat anymore. Did you have lunch today?"

"When?" Beckman asked sourly.

Wainwright came into the room then and stood there, staring at them bleakly.

"Something wrong?" Beckman asked.

"You two give me a pain."

"That's understandable," Masuto agreed.

"You got a kidnapping, and you treat it like a personal affair. You bust into a house in Los Angeles and maim two suspects, and you operate like this wasn't a police department and like you studied to be a pair of lunatics. This Clinton from the F.B.I. says you are arrogant and unreliable, and I'm inclined to agree with him."

"We couldn't reach you," Masuto said lamely.

"That's one lousy excuse. Suddenly you don't have a radio in your car. You knew goddamn well that I was over in the hotel with this Clinton guy, but you couldn't take five minutes to phone me. Oh, no. Now what the hell am I supposed to tell this guy? You got us involved in an international incident with these creeps from Washington crawling all over the place, and it don't help one bit for me to tell them that you kept their five lousy agronomists and a lot of plain citizens from being blown out of the sky. Oh, no. All they want to know is why they weren't informed of what was absolutely an F.B.I. matter, and what kind of a lousy, insubordinate police department do I run, and how come one of my cops nearly beats a suspect to death out of his own personal animosity?"

"I swear I only hit him once," Beckman protested. "Look at my hand!"

"Well, he's outside," Wainwright said.

"Who?"

"The F.B.I. guy, Clinton. And he wants to talk to you, Masao, and I don't want you giving him any lip or any of your goddamn Charlie Chan routine. You just listen to what he has to say, because we got trouble enough."

Masuto nodded, rose, and walked outside. Clinton was

sitting at a table, his attaché case open in front of him, writing. When he saw Masuto, he closed his notebook and rose to face the detective.

"So you finally condescend to speak to me, Sergeant Masuto. You had an appointment with me at eleven o'clock this morning, but you chose to ignore that—"

Now Wainwright and Beckman joined them, standing a few feet behind Masuto. Clinton went on talking.

"—and take matters into your own hand. You were involved in a kidnapping, but you saw no reason to report that to the F.B.I., and then you undertook an illegal search and seizure without a warrant or a court order, and then you and your partner gave a classic demonstration of police brutality. Well, just let me tell you this. That kind of thing is over. This matter is out of your hands. The man found dead in the pool at the Beverly Glen Hotel died of drowning accidentally. Both my government and the government of the Soviet Union concur in that decision, and you are to do nothing and say nothing to contradict this. Furthermore, Mrs. Stillman's murder of her husband will be treated and tried as an act of jealousy and revenge, and nothing will be said of her connection with the two Arabs. They will be deported, turned over to the German authorities, who have a prior claim and indictment against them. Nothing will be released on the attempt to destroy the airliner, and I have suggested to Captain Wainwright that he take measures concerning the insubordination of you and Detective Beckman. Now, do you understand this?"

Masuto nodded.

"Have you any comment?"

"Oh, yes, sir. Most humble apologies. So very sorry for

long and painful list of my ineptitudes. But must make one comment. It seems to me that you are one of the most incompetent and stupid men I have ever encountered, and you can stuff that right up your bureaucratic federal asshole."

And with that, Masuto turned on his heel and walked out. There was a long moment of silence, and then Beckman began to sputter.

"Get out of here!" Wainwright yelled.

Beckman fled. Clinton took a deep breath and said to Wainwright, "I want you to get rid of that man."

"Oh?"

"How can you run a police force, even a force like yours, with men like that?"

"I manage," Wainwright said.

"That insolent bastard! That damn Jap!"

"Hold on," Wainwright said coldly. "You turn my stomach, mister."

"What do you mean?"

"I mean he's an American. He's not Japanese. This is California, Mr. Clinton. We don't talk that way."

Clinton stared and Wainwright stared back.

"He's also a damn good cop," Wainwright said. "Maybe the best I got. I cooperated with you right down the line, and if you want to twist this filthy mess to your own ends, I got nothing to say about that. But right here you're on my turf. I don't come to Washington and tell you how to run your organization, and I'll thank you not to tell me how to run my police department. So let's finish up what we got and put this case away."

Masuto drove home to Culver City. He was tired. His mind had stopped functioning. Rage had wiped out any sense of achievement, and he felt lifeless.

He came into the house, and his son and daughter ran to greet him. They were in their pajamas, ready for bed, and Ana appeared to be none the worse for her experience. She had evidently informed Uraga of all the details of her kidnapping, and they both chattered away, excitedly. Masuto embraced them mechanically and listened without hearing. He was also very conscious of the fact that Kati had not come to greet him as he entered. Usually she was so anxious about his coming home that she would look for him through the window or listen for the sound of his car.

"Where is your mother?" he asked Uraga.

"In the kitchen."

"Go and play," he said to them. "I must talk to her."

He went into the kitchen. Kati stood at the sink, her back to him, cleaning shrimp and vegetables for tempura. She did not turn as he entered, and after a moment he went to her and kissed the bare spot on her shoulder.

"That will not help," she said coldly, without turning around.

"What have I done?"

"It's not what you have done. It's what you haven't done. Do you know what I went through today?"

He took her shoulders and turned her around to face him. "Don't you think I went thorugh the same thing?"

"Did you? Did you have to sit here and wait? And wait? Do you know what that is? Days go by and I don't see you and the children don't see you. Do you know what that is?

I'm not Japanese. I'm Nisei, as you are, but you treat me the way the Japanese men treat their wives."

"I don't. That's not fair."

"It is true, and you know it."

He shook his head helplessly. "I don't know what to say. I'm going to take a bath."

He was lying in the hot tub, the water as hot as his skin could bear, half asleep, relaxed for the first time in hours, when the door opened and Kati entered, carrying two huge fluffy white towels. She sat down beside the tub, the towels in her lap.

"Do you know, you are right," he said to her.

"I know I am."

"I saw you preparing tempura, so you can't be too angry at me."

"Ah, so. It's not because I am not angry, it's because I decided what to do."

"And what is that?"

"It concerns tomorrow, Saturday. Tomorrow, I will prepare a picnic lunch, and we will take the children and our bathing suits and we will drive up to Malibu and have a picnic on the beach, and the children will play all day in the sand and the water, and you and I will have an opportunity to resume our acquaintance."

"That would be wonderful." Masuto sighed. "But I have to go into the office and prepare my report."

"No," Kati said calmly. "You will call Captain Wainwright and tell him you cannot come in tomorrow. You can even lie to him, if you wish, and tell him that you are sick. You never use any of your sick time."

"I don't think Wainwright would appreciate that."

"But I would. So when you are out of the tub, you will

call Captain Wainwright."

Masuto thought about it. "It's too sudden to get sick. I would have to tell him the truth."

"Then you will tell him the truth. Then you can meditate if you wish, and then we will have your supper. I also have sushi."

"Why did you prepare my favorite food if you were so angry at me?" Masuto wondered.

"What has one thing got to do with the other?"

"Yes. I see. You are a remarkable woman, Kati."

After he had dried himself and put on his saffron-colored robe, he called the station and spoke to Wainwright.

"I just don't believe you," Wainwright said. "After the way you loused things up with the whole goddamn federal government?"

"It's either that or get a divorce."

"You give me one pain in the ass, Masao."

"Do I get the day off?"

"Take it, take it. It'll be a relief not to see you around for a whole weekend."

He put down the phone and turned to Kati, who stood there smiling.

"You see," she said, "it was very simple, wasn't it?"

He shook his head hopelessly.

"The children are in bed. Shall we eat?"

He nodded.

Later, heaping tempura onto his plate, she asked innocently, "What happened to the dancer?"

"She's in jail."

Kati smiled again. "Tomorrow will be a nice day," she said. "A married man should enjoy his wife and children."